JAN KOCHANOWSKI

SELECTED WORKS:
POETRY, DRAMA, PROSE

PUBLICATION SUBSIDIZED BY
THE POLISH BOOK INSTITUTE

BOOK INSTITUTE

THE ©POLAND
TRANSLATION
PROGRAM

©POLAND

SELECTED WORKS:

POETRY, DRAMA, PROSE

by Jan Kochanowski

Translated from the Polish and introduced by
Charles S. Kraszewski

This book has been published with the support
of the ©POLAND Translation Program

Publishers
Maxim Hodak & Max Mendor

Introduction © 2023, Charles S. Kraszewski

Cover art and illustration on page 6 © 2023, Max Mendor
© 2023, Glagoslav Publications
Book cover and interior book design by Max Mendor

Proofreading by Richard Coombes

www.glagoslav.com

ISBN: 978-1-80484-050-4
ISBN: 978-1-80484-051-1

First published by Glagoslav Publications in June 2023

A catalogue record for this book is available from the British Library.

JAN KOCHANOWSKI

SELECTED WORKS:
POETRY, DRAMA, PROSE

Translated from the Polish
and introduced by Charles S. Kraszewski

GLAGOSLAV PUBLICATIONS

CONTENTS

PROSE

Jan Kochanowski

(1530 – 1584)

Jan Kochanowski:

Poland's Shakespeare... and Marlowe, and Jonson, and Donne...

Charles S. Kraszewski

This title is something of a retread. In June, 2022, I used it to introduce the poet to the crowd assembled at the Guildhall in Stratford-upon-Avon following the dedication of Kochanowski's statue in the garden of Anne Hathaway's cottage. It is helpful and problematic at the same time. Helpful, because Jan Kochanowski is hardly a household name outside Poland — what name of any Polish poet, however deserving, is? — and it helps locate the bard from Czarnolas in period and significance for those coming across him for the first time. Kochanowski did have the same, if not greater, influence on the modern Polish literary idiom as Shakespeare had on the English; like Jonson, he was a *poeta doctus*, arguably a humanist of even wider horizons than Ben, given his university studies and travels; you might place him among the university wits of Marlowe and Greene and Nashe, and his Horatian pastorals smack of both Marlowe and Raleigh, while the often bawdy *Trifles*, especially those that sparkle with brilliant wordplay, simply beg comparison with Jack Donne. Problematical, not only because comparisons are odious, but it sets the bar of our expectations entirely too high. Unlike Shakespeare, for example, Kochanowski is the author of only one work for the stage — albeit a brilliant one — *The Dismissal of the Grecian Envoys*, and whereas he literally redefined the dry genre of the lament in his one work of truly pan-European significance — the *Threnodies*, written on the death of his little daughter Orszula — he left behind a rather modest collection of works. Of course, he died relatively young himself, at age fifty-four, and so, to continue with our British comparisons a few ages on, you can't expect the output of a Thomas Hardy from a person who lived only slightly longer than a Gerard Manley Hopkins.

It would be unjust to call Kochanowski a 'dabbler.' It is true that he set his hand to many literary genres, without concentrating his efforts in a single field; to continue our odious comparisons with the Elizabethans, whereas Shakespeare begins his career as a narrative poet and creates that noble series of sonnets, his fame rests upon thirty two-works for the stage, and in Marlowe's case, passing by Ovid and his few lyrics, he too is best known and justly lauded for seven great tragedies. Kochanowski, on the other hand, flitted from drama to Socratic dialogue, jocular trifle to lament, translations from the classics and the Bible to erudite prose (both what we might term cultural anthropology in his consideration of the myth of Czech and Lech to a treatise on Polish orthography). Of course, the great variety of his output testifies to an amazing breadth, a voracious intellect interested in every sort of literary expression. What is more worth noting: he excelled in them all. Who knows what later years would have brought, had death not stifled that restless artistic intellect before his sixth decade was quite passed? Of course that is an unanswerable question. We can only speak of what he's left behind — and most of that is magnificent.

It has become a commonplace to speak of Jan Kochanowski as the foremost Slavic poet of the Renaissance. Józef Magnuszewski, the great Polish comparatist, put this shorthand to a test: 'The statement that Kochanowski is the earliest creative talent of first-class quality in all Slavdom appeared rather late [here he cites a work by B. Chlebowski from 1883], and was repeated thereafter without more detailed development. Today, it has become common currency, although it still lacks a fuller foundation.'[1] In his short overview of the Slavic Renaissance poets, he finds that the closest to approach him, perhaps, is that 'most remarkable Czech latinist-poet Bohuslav Hasištejnský z Lobkovic,' who flourished a little earlier than Kochanowski (he died in 1510), the 'most personal character of whose lyrics express bitterness, sadness, and disenchantment, which tend towards Stoicism.' Yet, as he sees it, 'the Czech humanist had no desire of "becoming a national poet," but confined himself to the ambit of creativity in Latin.'[2] And so, despite the vibrant

---

1   Józef Magnuszewski, 'Twórczość Jana Kochanowskiego na tle poezji słowiańskiej XVI wieku,' in *Jan Kochanowski i Kultura Odrodzenia*, ed. by Zdzisław Libera and Maciej Żurowski (Warszawa: PWN, 1985), p. 121.

2   Magnuszewski, pp. 124–125.

CHARLES S. KRASZEWSKI

Renaissance traditions in Bohemia and Croatia, there truly is no indi-
vidual Slavic poet who attains a pan-European rank in many genres,
although he is mainly known in the West for one work, the *Threnodies.*

Jan Kochanowski was born in Sycyna, which is located a bit east of
centre in today's Poland. His father was a judge, and his mother, Anna
Białaczowska, was well-known enough as a person of refinement as
to be described in Łukasz Górnicki's *Dworzanin polski* [Polish Courtier, 1566] as a 'stately and very amusing lady.' The family was refined
indeed. Two of Kochanowski's brothers — Mikołaj and Andrzej — were
to enrich Polish literature with translations from the classics, *Plutarch's
Lives* and Virgil's *Aeneid*, respectively. His nephew Piotr (Mikołaj's son),
was to bring over Ariosto and Tasso into Polish.

Kochanowski was widely educated at universities both at home and
abroad. He attended the Jagiellonian University in Kraków and Prince
Albrecht's Academy at Königsberg (Królewiec, at the time), and the
University of Padua, where he served as *consiliarius* for the Polish 'nation'
studying there.[3] Although he remained faithful to the Catholic Church at
a time of religious controversy, he became familiar with Protestantism
in Königsberg[4] and — it seems — at Wittenberg, and his hymns have
been used by both denominations. He had powerful patrons, including
the magnate Jan Zamoyski, Bishop of Kraków Piotr Myszkowski, and
the aforementioned Albrecht, who, according to Jan Pilař, funded his
studies in Padua.[5] He also served for a while as royal secretary to King
Stefan Batory. But it is his estate in Czarnolas, which he praises so often
in his *Songs*, where he most enjoyed being — as he mentions more than
once in his works — and it is here where he accomplished that for which

---

3   Jadwiga Pietrusiewiczowa and Jadwiga Rytel, 'Jan Kochanowski,' in Zdzisław
Libera, et al., *Literatura Polska od średniowiecza do oświecenia* (Warsaw: PWN, 1988),
p. 91. Records of his time in Königsberg are sketchy. Although his brothers attended
university there, Kochanowski may have been less officially associated with the
school. He was, however, appreciated and patronised by Prince Albrecht.

4   Perhaps the fullest discussion of Kochanowski's reported stay in Königsberg
can be found in: Janusz Mattak, 'Jan Kochanowski in Königsberg,' *Jahrbücher für
Geschichte Osteuropas*, Vol. 36, No. 3 (1988), pp. 341–349.

5   Jan Pilař, *Má cesta za polskou poezjí* (Praha: Československý spisovatel, 1981),
p. 143. Mattak (pp. 344–345) gives a fuller account of the still-extant correspondence on this topic between Kochanowski and Albrecht in the spring of 1556; Albrecht granted Kochanowski a stipend of fifty Prussian marks for the Italian journey.

we are most grateful: his poetry, and it is that poetry which lifted his Czarnolas out of the geographical atlases and into common parlance as a metaphor of poetic excellence.[6]

It is frequently mentioned that Kochanowski made the acquaintance of Pierre Ronsard. Czesław Miłosz posits their meeting in Paris, before the Polish poet's return to his homeland in 1559.[7] This should not surprise anyone who remembers that Milton was for many years arguably better known in Italy than in his homeland, or that Sarbievius, whom we mention below, went on to influence poets as far afield, both nationally and confessionally, as Coleridge and Isaac Watts. Latin was the lingua franca of educated Europe — much as English is today. For those who like to speak of influence, there is a tantalising fragment from poem I.15 of the *Songs*:

> Place not your trust in smooth cheeks, fondling hands —
> That were to build your house on shifting sands.
> The sun that shines at dawn at dusk will set,
> And as the wrinkles grow, so does regret.
>
> You'll age, decline, you blink, and... have you died?
> With so few to lament at your graveside?
> Ah, such a friend I wished to be for you,
> Except that your tears should my grave bedew.
>
> (21–28)

The reader of Ronsard might catch an echo of the similarly elegiac 'Quand vous seras bien vielle,' with its gentle remonstrance of the woman who spurns the narrator in her youth, only to remember him with longing in her lonely old age. Did Kochanowski know this poem? It seems unlikely — Ronsard's sonnet first saw the light of day in print in 1578, while Kochanowski had returned from his student years in Europe almost twenty-five years before. But the spirit blows where it lists, and

---

6   In Polish, when a young poet is mentioned as being 'on his way to Czarnolas,' it means the same as having him ascend Mount Helicon.

7   Czesław Miłosz, *The History of Polish Literature* (Berkeley: University of California Press, 1983), p. 61.

CHARLES S. KRASZEWSKI

there is no reason to wonder at similar ideas occurring to born poets of the same time period, and the same general humanistic background.

POETA DOCTUS

Whether poets are born or made, they cannot help but be formed by their experiences and education. In the case of Jan Kochanowski, born into a well-to-do and refined family of the lesser aristocracy, and educated throughout Europe, this means being formed by the classical, and especially Horatian, tradition.

Allusions to classical myth are sprinkled throughout his poems. In song 5 from book I of the *Songs*, for example, he makes an unforced allusion to Alexander the Great in a musing on the benefits of moderation:

> The King of Macedon,
> For a brief moment won
> The world entire. Yet still he thought it rough
> To have so little — one world was not enough,
>   (15–16)

expecting his reader, quite reasonably, to be familiar with the same stories he is. Speaking of mythological allusions in the *Threnodies*, Ray J. Parrott, Jr. makes this very point:

> Through the use of mythological and classical allusions, Kochanowski has succeeded in identifying his mental anguish with a series of classical figures who experienced similar grief. This poetic association, again, reinforces his own image of grief to an emphatic degree for the reader. The reader 'perceives' and can empathise with the poet's emotion of grief through the common medium of the mythological or classical allusion. Heraclitus, Simonides, Niobe, and Orpheus: these names evoke a specific response in the sensitive reader acquainted with the rich classical and mythological traditions, and serve to realise Kochanowski's grief upon the reader through a transferral of associations.[8]

---

8   Ray J. Parrott Jr. 'Mythological Allusions in Kochanowski's *Laments*,' *The Polish Review*, Vol. 14, No. 1 (1969), p. 14.

Although, as I reckon, more than one college professor of today would confirm, such things cannot be taken for granted of the students ranged before him, Kochanowski comes from a time that unabashedly and naturally assented to ideas such as Christendom — modern Europe emerging from the Mediterranean past, accepted and transformed by Christianity. Trifle 95 from book II, 'On Rome' is written, not so much in praise of the old Empire itself — Kochanowski is satisfied with his Poland as a political entity; he does not mourn the fall of unified Imperial authority as, for example, Dante did — as it is in praise of Latin culture, the glue that bonds together the nations of the continent. For him, the great gift that has been, and must be, preserved, is the Latin language:

> As every nation bowed before the right
> Of Rome to rule — as long as she had might —
> So now, tripped up, she shivers and she frets,
> Perceiving on all sides new mortal threats.
> Much better fares her tongue, which men still praise;
> Ash yields spear-shafts; the best fruit — comes from bays.

This poem is something of an amplified confirmation of Horace's claims to immortality in Ode III:30, where he (again, quite rightly) asserts that his fame will endure *dum Capitolium / scandet cum tacita virgine Pontifex*[9] [as long as the Pontifex will ascend the steps of the Capitol along with the silent virgin] — which proved a modest boast, as it still endures today, long after the fall of Roman religion and Rome itself and even — alas — a universal familiarity with Europe's common tongue.

And so, Kochanowski the *poeta doctus* makes frequent and easy allusions to the Greek and Roman classics in his work. Reuel K. Wilson makes an interesting comment in regard to the naturalness of Kochanowski's erudition: 'Although he too wrote "learned" poetry, Kochanowski's imagination was less bookish than Ronsard's.' Whatever the case may be (and here Wilson is referring to Kochanowski's talent in recreating translated texts so that they 'sound Polish')[10] he is fairly 'bookish' in his lyrics: in I.6 he tries to convince a girl to stay

---

9   Horace, Ode XXX, Book III, 'Exegi monumentum...', 8–9.

10   Reuel K. Wilson, 'Kochanowski and Ronsard: Contemporaries and Kindred Spirits,' *The Polish Review,* Vol. 22, No. 1 (1977), p. 22.

with him by rehearsing the fate of Europa; in I.21 and II.2 he compares himself to the legendary poets Amphion, Orpheus, and Arion; in the *Threnodies* he refers to Heraclitus, Simonides, Orpheus, Sappho, Cicero, and the ever-brooding myth of Persephone. He enriches the Polish language with translations from the Latin and the Greek. Trifles II.32 and III.25 are translations from the Greek Anthology; he also translates Anacreon (fittingly, for the *Trifles*), a portion of Homer in the 'Monomachia of Paris and Menelaus' (to say nothing of his reworking of a small segment of *Iliad* III into an entire play, *The Dismissal of the Grecian Envoys*); and even began a translation of Euripides' *Alcestis*, which, to our eternal regret, he abandoned after just one hundred lines.

As we say above, this is neither pompous nor forced; it is natural for a poet composing in an age when his readers emerged from the same educational background as he. As Wacław Walecki states in his discussion of the *Dismissal of the Grecian Envoys*, 'the spiritual atmosphere of the era prompted Kochanowski to write a tragedy that refers to a well-known historical theme in order to give it a universal, human, timeless meaning.'[11] Kochanowski is no mere devotee of tradition. In his long narrative poem *The Satyr*, we come across this passage speaking of pedagogy. Following a long dissertation on proper behaviour, both political and personal:

> 'You didn't learn
> That in the woods!' You'll say, but I in turn:
> 'No, you're mistaken.' For indeed I did!
> All this I have from Chiron, strange hybrid
> Of man and horse, tutor of Achilles,
> Whose school was a cave sunk amidst the trees —
> Rustic academy, for sure! And yet
> He lagged behind no professor in wit.

> (330–337)

---

11   Wacław Walecki, 'Aus der Geschichte des altpolnischen Dramas (I. "Die Abfertigung der griechischen Sendboten" von Jan Kochanowski),' *Wiener Slavistisches Jahrbuch*, Vol. 33 (1987), p. 169.f.

The mention of Chiron is both a Classical reference, and something more. Achilles' schooling did not take place at any sort of Platonic academy, but in the deep forest, under the tutelage of a creature that is both man and beast. In short, Kochanowski would suggest that the classical tradition is open to all — common sense. This is the complement to another passage to be found in the same poem, where the Wild-Man considers theology. Simple Christianity, he states, such as he learned in the woods from hermits, is more valuable than all the 'demagoguery' of Prague, Geneva, or Trent, for that matter.

It was to be a somewhat later poet of Poland — the Baroque Jesuit Maciej Kazimierz Sarbiewski ('Sarbievius,' 1595–1640), who would win fame throughout Europe as 'the Christian Horace,' but Kochanowski too both imitates, and incarnates, the Horatian ideal in his poetry. In fact, Maria Cytowska credits him with being the father of Horatian poetry in Polish: 'Before Kochanowski, the Latinate Polish elegy drew its inspirations from the works of Ovid [...]. Kochanowski was our first Polish Horatian. As the "Horatius Polonus," he is worthy of being set alongside Jean Salmon Macrin (1480–1557), the French Horace.'[12] Song I.2, an adaptation from a Horatian ode, sings the praises of the simple, honest life that the Roman poet professed:

> Yet no rejoicing surpasses the supreme
> Tranquility of him with conscience clean,
> Who, searching through his heart no shame there finds
> With which to call to fault a reckless mind.
>
> (17–20)

And true to both Classical and Catholic tradition, Kochanowski never rejects the pleasures of the flesh

> Good thought, whose company no man can lure
> Though he have silk-hung walls and golden door,
> Contemn not this my shady bower-plot
> Though I be sober, or by drink besot.
>
> (23–32)

---

12   Maria Cytowska, 'Kochanowski a Antyk (Tradycjonalizm czy nowatorstwo?),' in Libera and Żurowski, p. 96.

Although one of his prose tracts is a polemic against habitual drunkenness, here Kochanowski — like the Horace of the *carpe diem* odes — acknowledges the joys of imbibing *usque ad hilaritatem* as naturally as he sprinkles his classical erudition through his poems. Indeed, Horatian praise of moderation is no poetic affectation for Kochanowski, it is a rule of life. Note, for example, this passage from the Platonic dialogue 'Guesses:'

> So modestly did the Polish kings of those days live, that the simplest farmer would be ashamed to live so today. What are we to think of the carriage of the common men, when such was that of the kings? It's easy to see that people did not find their happiness or self-respect in long dinners and foreign drink, but rather in sobriety and moderation, so necessary to a chivalric people. There is no reason for us to be surprised at the fact that the old kings lived lives of moderation, and, consequently, the common people did so as well, in comparison to the wasteful times of today, for they held in contempt, as a stain upon the Republic, those things which we vaunt today. And as to their nobility of character — this I would not wish to assay in comparison with us.

This fits in with the classical ideal of the golden mean, repeated again and again in the odes of Horace, and frequently bewailed by him as well as neglected in the present day. The French critic Jacques Langlade provides an exhaustive list of the virtues especially venerated by Kochanowski, rooting them in the classical tradition. Although he may exaggerate a bit with his insistence on the 'distinctness' of Kochanowski's system from Christian thought, and nearly makes him a Pelagian as far as moral theology goes, it is worth citing the list in full:

> The qualities that Kochanowski most appreciated were: sobriety, disdain of money and luxury, simplicity, sweetness, and justice, devotion to the common good, courage, and the spirit of sacrifice. His ideal is not contrary to the Christian ideal, but it is distinct therefrom. One finds neither the dogma of the fall of man and original sin in his system, nor the spirit of fear and humility, nor a preoccupation with divine grace,

with inquietude concerning the Beyond. The poet believes the human should be capable of realising the Good through his own forces alone; to practise virtue and to assure himself of eternal life. As can be seen, we are far from Catholicism, and even farther from Calvinism here; while on the contrary, we are very close to Gorgias, *Phédon*, and the *Dream of Scipio*.[13]

Evidence enough for Kochanowski's traditional religiosity may be found in his works; we will see him struggling with 'inquietude concerning the Beyond' in the *Threnodies*, for example, along with implicit references to man's innate bent toward evil — the classical residue of original sin. But be that as it may, it is worth stressing Kochanowski's debt to Mediterranean culture, which played just as formative a role in his intellectual makeup as the Church. Wiktor Weintraub is closer to a just assessment of the balance of Classicism and Christianity in Kochanowski's works in his discussion of Song II.25, the justly-famed hymn 'Czego chcesz od nas, Panie, za Twe hojne dary?' [What dost Thou ask of us O Lord, for Thy abundant treasure?]:

> It would be difficult to find another 16th-century Polish poem so representative of the Renaissance ethos and the Renaissance style. It is, no doubt, a religious poem, written in praise of God. But it is also a poem written in praise of this world, its magnificence, beauty and harmony. Of course, compared with God, the earth can be called 'lowly,' nevertheless in its perfection it reflects God's greatness and benevolence. In Kochanowski's poem, God is being adored through His creation. The whole poem is infused with deep optimism.[14]

None of this is incompatible with the Christian tradition, of course, and to say what Weintraub asserts here is as much as saying that Kochanowski draws inspiration as much from St Ambrose of Milan — whose great

---

13   Jacques Langlade, 'Jan Kochanowski: L'humaniste,' *Revue des Etudes Slaves*, Vol. 10, No. 1/2 (1930), p. 53.

14   Wiktor Weintraub, 'Kochanowski's Renaissance Manifesto,' *The Slavonic and East European Review*, Vol. 30, No. 75 (1952), p. 413.

hymns offer just such effusive praise of God through his creation — as he does from Cicero.

Moderation, sobriety, the middle road — these are all paired, in Kochanowski's work as in that of Horace, with manliness, courage, and the physical and mental readiness necessary to rise to the defence of one's homeland when the need arises. Although every generation tends to look back on the 'old days' as an exemplar, unreachable by 'degenerate' contemporary society, the motif of the nefarious cancer of luxury — peace misused — which is found in Horace's 'Roman Odes,' is present in Kochanowski's *Songs* as well:

> Dear God! Are we of such fathers — stout, brave —
> Degenerate spawn? Spinning in their grave
> They must be! Sacred peace! Thou hast one vice:
> With thee, brawn turns to flab, and in a trice!
> (I.13:17–20)

If Poland has suffered any setbacks in her struggles against the rising power of Muscovy in the East, it is due to this: the degenerate modern youth who no longer prepare for war in times of peace, and their elders, who are no better, abandoning chivalric exercise for filthy lucre. According to the Satyr, it is the desire for wealth that has distracted the Poles' attention from the defence of their country:

> In Poland there's none but merchant and broker.
> For cattle sold in Brzeg, who's the most cash?
> To Gdańsk, who's ferried the most grain or ash?
> Such are your laurels! While — look to the East:
> There you'll spy Tatars, fiercer than any beast!
> (34–38)

Whether or not bribery and greed were such dire problems in Kochanowski's day as they were to become later, when venal senators and representatives to Parliament were corrupted by agents of neighbouring empires to abuse the *liberum veto*, through which any man present could table any matter before the Sejm by merely rising from his seat and declaring 'I disagree,' they are a constant theme in Kochanowski's writing. They constitute the main theme of Ulysses' angry speech in *The*

Dismissal of the Grecian Envoys, following the corrupt Trojan Senate's refusal to restore Helen to her husband:

> O lawless kingdom, near calamity!
> Where neither truth is loved, nor righteousness
> Has place, but all stinks of the market square!
> Where wastrels such as this, with metal chips
> Can win the most exalted of the land
> To paint his lechery a virtue, gild
> His scoundrel's burglary a patriotic quest!
>
> (IV:5–11)

Along with the danger to the state that arises from greed, there is also the matter of hypocrisy, moved toward the end of the cited passage. Kochanowski, true to his classical roots, is a devotee of personal virtue. As he puts it in his 'Essay on Virtue,'

> Two things, therefore, ennoble man: manners and intelligence. Manners come from the virtues, and reason from study; both of these things contain something invaluable to man. But if only one of these is to remain a man, let it be virtue he holds to, rather than learning. For learning without virtue is like a sword in the hands of a madman: he harms himself as well as others. Virtue, though it be accompanied by nothing else, is praiseworthy and useful.

With excusable exaggeration, Kochanowski sets virtue and piety at the keystone of the foundation of the Polish kingdom, which he elaborates in the patriotic ode which is song 10 of Book I:

> God abhors falsehood and loves righteousness.
> this the wheelwright Piast bears sure witness,
> For he resides in Heaven, who Poland
> Ruled with just hand.
>
> Ziemowit stands to the right of his sire,
> Equal to all, but you, Mieszko, stand higher,

> Who with Christ's waters of regeneration
> Laved your nation.

(33–40)

It seems that, unlike Rome, Paris, and Britain, Poland did not have the luxury (or the obligation) of finding a protagonist for its foundational myth amongst the heroes fleeing Troy aflame. Rather, he mines Polish folklore for the myth of Piast's miraculous elevation to the first Polish throne, but that Cincinnatian ideal that he represents in the North is certainly coloured by Mediterranean culture — just as the early Polish chronicles supplement the meagre knowledge of the pagan religion of the Slavs by inserting a Venus here and a Mars there.

The praise of Mieszko, on the other hand, as the first Polish ruler to Christianise his people is historical fact: the baptism of his people, which is generally considered as the baptism 'of Poland,' took place in 965. Ever since then, Poland has defined herself as a Latin Christian nation, and the inheritor of the Mediterranean culture that stretches back beyond the Christianisation of Rome herself. Kochanowski buys into the ancient Greek division of the world into 'civilised' and 'barbarian' — locating among the latter the Islamic powers of Turkey and Crimea against whom Poland was constantly doing battle. In II:5, another poem in which Kochanowski strikes the Horatian tone of the degeneracy of the flabby contemporary Poles, he castigates them not only for their martial softness, but also for not living up to their mission as the 'antemurale Christianitatis.'

> By bandits we're raided, by bandits killed,
> Who neither city firm nor village build,
> But pitch their rugs upon our meadows, where
> Us they consume, disordered, unprepared!
>
> Thus on the scattered flocks prey wolves at will,
> Fearing no shepherd as they tear and kill;
> The shepherd's gone. He's far away from here
> And no one leads the valiant sheepdogs near.
>
> If we cannot oppose such flimsy men,
> If we so swell their courage, Poles, what then?

They've all but set upon our throne their king —
Consider that! And feel you not the sting?
(13–24)

Nor is this directed only at his peers. More than once, Kochanowski underscores the responsibility of rulers to set a good example, for as they act, their subjects often follow. The greatest example of this message is an extended one: his one and only complete play.

THE DISMISSAL OF THE GRECIAN ENVOYS

This rather brief dramatic work was written to be performed at the wedding festivities of Crown Sub-chancellor Jan Zamoyski, a patron of Kochanowski's, and Krystyna Radziwiłłówna, which took place on 12 January 1578.[15] Unlike the Elizabethan drama, which derives from the Latin stage, the *Dismissal of the Grecian Envoys* is based on the classical Greek model, with scenes alternating with choral odes. One of these, Ode II, is an admonishment to rulers to act rightly, as the eyes of all are always upon them. As Priam and the Trojan nobility file into the senate to debate whether or not to return Helen to her aggrieved husband, they plead:

Let them take care, for when the vulgar sins,
The cancer of his crime ends where it begins.
But when a leader's crimes burst into bloom,
Whole cities and whole empires fall to ruin.
(II:17–20)

At the time in which the play was written, Poland, under King Stefan Batory, was facing a threat from the rising power of Ivan the Terrible's Muscovy in the east. Polish fiefs in modern Estonia and Latvia were threatened by Muscovite expansion, and it has been traditional to see in the *Dismissal* — especially in the ominous prophecy of Cassandra, and Antenor's warning to the King at the conclusion of the play — a call to arms: prepare for war, now, while there's still time, and the enemy has not yet set foot upon our soil. But a much more interesting theme is that

---

15   In Jazdów, at the time a village just outside Warsaw. Fittingly, the Institute of Theatre is located in this parkland, which now forms part of the city of Warsaw.

CHARLES S. KRASZEWSKI

of virtue and personal responsibility, which Kochanowski derives from his classical and Christian background. In short, if everyone, especially rulers, do exactly what they should do, and not what would be to their personal advantage, or what would be easier or cheaper to do, the kingdom would stand secure, no matter the threat.

And yet that's exactly what Priam does *not* do. As he charges the Trojan senators with debating the Helen issue, he ends with: 'Troy, / Whatever twist you give the rudder, I / Will trust the ship of state into your hands' (III:28–30). Really? What if they decide to lay hands on Ulysses and Menelaus, spurning the ancient right of diplomatic immunity, and slay them on the spot? What if they decide to sacrifice Helen, out of spite, putting her to death in front of her husband? 'Whatever twist they give the rudder?' Kochanowski's Priam, just like Homer's Priam and Virgil's Latinus too, for that matter, is a weak king. A king is not there to count votes. He is anointed of God, and his prerogative, his duty, is to make decisions regardless of what the majority say — consulting the eternal balance of Good and Evil rather than the ballot urns. It is for this reason that in his disquisition on kingship St Thomas Aquinas finds monarchy both the best, and worst, system of government. It is best when the King realises that he is bound to act in line with God's will — doing what is right on behalf of his people. It is worst when a tyrant misuses his power and exploits his people for his own purposes.

Priam is a tyrant, not a king, when he bows to the unjust arguments of the majority:

> 'I would have been glad, had unanimity
> Been the outcome of these consultations,
> But, despite the lack of concord, I must,
> As sovereign ruler of the realm of Troy
> Abide your will and accordingly find
> In Paris' favour, charging thus the Greeks
> To forfeit Helen in Medea's place.'
>
> (III:187–194)

No, he 'mustn't' do anything, except what is right! When he finally realises that the destruction of his city now looms, thanks not only to his son's theft of someone else's wife, and reflecting on a dire prophecy received when Paris was but a baby, he exclaims:

> Would I had the whelp exposed!
> The wolves should long ago have torn apart
> The embryonic sin, and spread its bones
> Upon the hills.
>
> (Epilogue, 16–19)

It's too late for that now. But it wasn't too late, just hours before, when he was able to follow the dictates of justice and return Helen. His sin is just as great, if not greater, than that of Paris. Aleksander Sroczyński sums this up magnificently in his statement that, in Kochanowski's *Dismissal*, 'Troy is the paradigm of a rotten polity.'[16]

But we must remember that — for good or ill — Poland was not an absolutist monarchy. Magnuszewski reminds us:

> Kochanowski's Renaissance poetry matured in times when the development and suppleness of the young Polish culture, broadly open to the, in effect, sublime European currents, progressed in step with the blossoming of statehood, which at the time took the form of a republic covering large swathes of land; a noble republic, but one that, considering the European conditions of the time, ensured the participation of a large portion of the society in public life. All of this élan aroused the creative strengths of the Polish poet, providing him with wings.[17]

The king was elected, and it was the nobles who held all the power in parliament. Kochanowski, who also understood the dangers of this sort of situation, here seems to offer a defence of the *liberum veto*. For, as the messenger relates the discussions at the Senate, we learn that both Ukalegon and Antenor had stood up to disagree with the sentiment of the majority, led by the glib 'two-wrongs-make-a-right' Paris, and urged the return of Helen to her husband. Had this been Poland, only one such

---

16   Aleksander Sroczyński, 'We Were the Trojans: Rhetoric and Political Community in Medieval and Early Modern Sarmatia and Illyria,' in *Premodern Rulership and Contemporary Political Power: The King's Body Never Dies*, ed. by Karolina Mroziewicz and Aleksander Sroczyński (Amsterdam: Amsterdam Univ. Press, 2017), p. 181.

17   Magnuszewski, p. 129.

voice would have been necessary to table the unjust motion and avert catastrophe. If, as Janusz Pelc asserts, 'the hero is actually the people as a whole,'[18] they constitute a tragic hero, foiled by their leaders, dragged into misfortune powerlessly, against their will.

It's too bad that 'Poland's Shakespeare' wrote but one play. He had a talent for dramatic composition, which can be seen not only in the surviving fragment of his translation of Euripides' *Alcestis*, but also from a consideration of Trifle I.79, 'On a Spanish Doctor.' In this little gem, a satisfyingly full dramatic scene is presented in the space of just fourteen lines, shared out in crisp parts between four voices, including that of the narrator. Here, Kochanowski's talent as editor or director is seen in heading in the other direction — concision — from that which we find in the *Dismissal*, which is the amplification of just thirty lines of Homer's *Iliad* into a full dramatic work.

KOCHANOWSKI AND RELIGION

To return for a moment to Kochanowski's ideal of a well-governed state, not only virtue and the old manly, republican virtues are necessary, but unanimity in religion is needed to cement together the body politic. This is the point that the Priest would drive home to the landowner over the course of the Platonic dialogue — also a dramatic form of a sort — called 'Guesses:'

> For the praise of God results in this, that when all confess to and heed the Lord God in the same manner, we receive of Him not only ghostly blessings, according to the promises He made unto us, but our Republic, on account of unity, becomes a firm defence in this world for ourselves and our descendants.

One wonders to which side of the controversy concerning the Established Church in England Kochanowski would have inclined, had he been a Londoner. Would he have been a recusant, as some suggest Shakespeare was, or would he have acknowledged the Elizabethan settlement? It is a fair question, as in the same work he unabashedly

---

18   Janusz Pelc, 'Przemiany świadomości poetyckiej Jana Kochanowskiego,' in Libera and Żurowski, p. 69.

upholds the Church as a sure support of order, an aid to the state, not a rival, and certainly not anything to be separated from it:

> For just as when an impoverished householder invites a perceptive, wealthy guest to his home, the latter will arrive with gifts that both cheer his host and give witness to his own generosity and honesty, so the Lord God, comprehending that in this well-ordered community, not only is human security made all the more firm, but His praise is also more solidly established, He supports and ensures human laws and legislated customs with His own revelations and teachings. For we cannot call any republic firmly-grounded and well-ordered where people carry out their duties out of terror of the punishments threatened by the law — for they might sin in order to avoid such punishment. Rather, only there do we find security and good government where, not out of fear, but because of their virtue, people do what they ought. For such as wish both to avoid punishment and do good will never do wrong — and such is the effect that the faith has upon them. Therefore it can be remarked that a proper republic rests more certainly upon faith than upon law.

He did not cotton to the religious conflicts of the age of Reformation, which often boiled over into bloodshed among Christians. This he too castigates in the manner of Lysistrata. In short, where brothers fall out, no one wins except the foreign enemy lurking without, just waiting for both to be weakened sufficiently to pounce upon them:

> We not only be torn asunder in secular matters, we must differ in things of the spirit as well, tearing ourselves apart into strange and various faiths, which introduce all the more contention among the people! And let us consider that all the wars that in olden days the Christians waged against the pagans arose from nothing other than differences in faith. And these Christian armies, and those forces of the orders of darkness, never fought so furiously over Jerusalem or Constantinople — with Turks and Saracens! — as the Christians today do over Christ and His faith!

CHARLES S. KRASZEWSKI

This is a message that his countryman Sarbievius would make a few decades later, in Latin odes directed at the warring Christian powers of Europe.

Yet Kochanowski's religion is broad minded enough for him to suggest in his most famous hymn that God is the 'property' of no single sect or demonic nation: 'The Church encompasses Thee not, the world is full of Thee' (Songs, II.25:3). He is sober enough to recognise the failings of the Catholic Church; see, for example Trifles I.44 'On the Holy Father' and II.19 'On a Priest,' in which he castigates the moral failings of the Catholic clergy, from simple chaplain to the Pope himself, with all the snide invective of his Protestant colleague Mikołaj Rej.[19] Although Kochanowski never abandons the Catholic faith, his ideal of a 'true Christian' has a lot of the emphasis on primitive belief that motivated the early Protestants. He is 'not / An orator or learned polyglot, / But one who keeps God's precepts all his days. (*The Satyr*, 204-205) It is a simple, primitive Christianity that he praises, something that characterises the honest, simple believer, whether Protestant, Orthodox or Catholic, both the illiterate woman at Mass repeating her rosary and the illiterate peasant in the field who pauses to recite the Angelus at noon:

> I studied neither in Leipzig nor Prague,
> Nor listened to Genevan demagogue
> Explain the faith; all that I've understood
> I gleaned from hermits living in deep wood
> And barren mountain summit, who impart
> The sort of faith that takes root in the heart.
>
> (221–226)

It is also the simple trust of the (formerly) chivalric nobility, who had the custom of partially unsheathing the sword at their side during the reading of the Gospel at Mass, as a sign that they were ready to defend it to the death:

---

19   In connection with Kochanowski's Protestant sympathies, Janusz Mattak points out the 'lack of Marian motifs and cult of the Saints in the poet's work.' See Mattak, p. 344. All the same, Jacques Langlade points out, with some justice, that 'the Reformation succeeded not in conquering Kochanowski, nor to mark his faith with any sensible nuance.' See Langlade, p. 40.

Such a good Christian I will ever praise.
          If your view of these things is different,
Show what you're made of! Off with you to Trent!
          Tell me, how did the old Poles grip the sword
Upon hearing the Gospel of the Lord?
          You think they wasted much time in debate?
(But that's a horny syllogism, hard to explicate).
          Here's what they thought: 'These truths are beyond me.
It's not for me to plumb God's mysteries.
          But once made whole by Baptism's sacred laver
My duty is to serve my loving Saviour.
          I know His Word, to Him I owe my all;
In Him I'll stand fast, till in death I fall.'
          Tell him his faith is faulty! Soon you'll see
Why I would rather stand with such as he!
                                        (206–220)

KOCHANOWSKI AND WOMEN

If it is seventeenth century British parallels we are looking for, Kochanowski seems most similar to Donne in respect to women. From their
biographies, we know both men to have been good, loving husbands
and fathers, and acknowledgements of their passion and attachment
can be found in more than one of their poems. Enforced separation
from one's wife — and considering the travel possibilities of the day,
these tended to be long separations — were a fact of life for any man
engaged in government or service to great men, in which both Donne
and Kochanowski were engaged. The English reader will recall to
mind Donne's great 'Valedictions,' especially that 'Forbidding Mourning,' with its marvellous metaphysical conceits of 'gold to an airy thin-
ness beat' and the supreme image of husband and wife as two legs of
one compass. As for Kochanowski, we may point out some lines from
the end of his jocular poetic epistle to Bishop Myszkowski of Kraków,
in which the poet chides his patron for holding him so long away from
his wife:

Re-join what you have deigned to separate.
'Tis in your power to better the sad state

Of loving hearts, which you apart have forced,
That would not die, as now they live, divorced!

(II.20:29–32)

This is a different sort of poetics than Donne's serious valedictions, but it is built on a clever conceit that the English metaphysical would certainly appreciate. For it is a Donne-like paradox, accusing the Bishop of divorcing, rather than uniting, the married pair; the reference to Christ's 'What God has joined, let no man separate' is a bit of strong, fitting humour, which would not work so well in its teasing irony if the recipient were not a priest.

Donne would also appreciate, and perhaps be jealous of, the poetic craft that went into Kochanowski's most famous poem on women, Trifle I.4, 'Raki' [Crabs]. The title is a subtle hint to the reader on how to read the ingenious joke. Because Polish, like Latin and Greek, is a highly inflected language, word order is a much freer affair than it is in a non-inflected language like English. Kochanowski makes brilliant use of the nature of the Polish language in order to create a poem that can be read perfectly both left to right, and right to left. Here are lines five and six of this poem in the original Polish:

Miłują z serca, nie patrzają zdrady,
Pilnują prawdy, nie kłamają rady.

The five couplets that make up the whole rhyme at both the conclusion and the beginning of each line, and the negative particle *nie* [no, not, don't] is placed at the very middle of each line, right after the caesura, and serves as a kind of pivot to the entire verse. So, read left to right: *Miłują z serca, nie patrzają zdrady*, or 'they love from the heart, they do not look to betray,' can be flipped to read *Zdrady patrzają, nie z serca miłują*, or 'They look to betray, they do not love from the heart.' Likewise, *Pilnują prawdy, nie kłamają rady* 'they guard the truth, they do not lie gladly' can be spun into its opposite: *Rady kłamają, nie prawdy pilnują*: 'they gladly lie, it's not the truth they guard,' and so on, all throughout the poem. Left to right, praise of women, right to left... While Jadwiga Pietrusiewiczowa and Jadwiga Rytel probably go a bit too far in describing the *Trifles* as 'An intimate, lyric memoir of the author,' it is hard to disagree with their statement that, in them, 'Kochanowski stretched the limits of what poetry might become.'[20]

This was a different age; perhaps neither better nor worse than our own, but people certainly had thicker skin, and no one got too upset about stereotypical humour. Women can be butts of Jan Kochanowski's jokes, and even when he is not joking, as in the case of the narrator of Song I.15, who blames a lover for fickleness in deciding to leave him, he employs stereotype:

> I won't oppose you. What more can I say?
> I only wonder at the curious way
> Of women — so unstable! With each wind
> Like well-greased weathercocks, one sees them spin.
> (5–8)

He is a man of his times; he appreciates women, as his age taught him to do: as man's helpmeet, nothing more:

> On fields of battle one may win great glory,
> In time of peace, by stirring oratory,
> But if a man's adorned not by a wife
>   Futile is his life.
> (II.10:1–4)

But we might also say: nothing less. Although gender roles have changed quite a bit since Kochanowski's days, and modern women (and men) might roll their eyes at his praiseful evaluation of an honest woman's breeding/mothering capabilities:

> She bears him a hale brood of girls and boys,
> Each like their father, each a font of joys.
> No need to search through distant kin for heir:
>   He's enough to spare,
> (17–20)

---

20   Jadwiga Pietrusiewiczowa and Jadwiga Rytel, 'Jan Kochanowski,' in Zdzisław Libera, et al., *Literatura Polska od średniowiecza do oświecenia* (Warsaw: PWN, 1988), pp. 97, 98.

CHARLES S. KRASZEWSKI

she's more than just that. In this poem filled with praise of women (however dated some of it might sound) he appreciates the good wife in the creation and management of his wealth:

> Of shrewd economy manors are made.
> Others amass great wealth through prudent trade.
> But with no wife to aid him? Have no fear:
> Watch it disappear.
>
> (5–8)

It is unfair to judge people who lived long ago by the standards of the present age. We shouldn't expect a Jan Kochanowski or a John Donne to look at the roles of women in society as we do in the twenty-first century. It is, all the same, a mark of his broad understanding for half the human race that, in a poem such as II.10 quoted above, he raises woman above mere subordination to man — Milton's infamous 'He for God only, she for the God in him' — to the position of a partner in the proper running of the home economy. As he puts it, he who is not 'adorned with a good wife' lives in vain.

There is, however, one role for woman that Jan Kochanowski never thought of writing about: that of the keening mother, mourning the loss of her child. Nor was he prepared for it himself. Vanitas themes and the *memento mori* are to be found threaded throughout his writing. But in all these, for one example, the Horatian Song I.5, the treatment of death is formulaic — serious perhaps, but devoid of immediacy, a paper tiger:

> For death — today remote,
> Soon grabs all by the throat:
> The richest magnate and the meanest slave
> Settle accounts outstanding in the grave.
>
> (21–24)

All this was suddenly to change with the death of his little daughter Orszula. Death is no longer a distant eventuality that can be handled in light moralising verse, but a fierce and pitiless enemy to the grieving father and mother who helplessly watch their child die:

Just so the dragon, scenting covert nest
Slinks near with greedy maw, on slimy breast
To snatch the chicks, the while the nightingale,
Helpless, sends up an anguished mother's wail;

The poor thing hops, and battles, in panicked strife —
In vain, hardly escaping with her life.

(Threnody I:9–14)

THE *THRENODIES*

I feel it incumbent upon me to warn the reader that we are about to embark upon a long discussion of Kochanowski's most famous work, of which I am unable to speak without going into a rather detailed reading. I'm rather surprised by this myself. For throughout my acquaintance with the poetry of Jan Kochanowski, which goes back some forty years now, I've always passed over the *Threnodies* to zero in on the *Trifles* and the *Dismissal of the Grecian Envoys*. I'm discovering no America here when I say that our personal predilections predispose our tastes in literature; I've always been fascinated with theatre and wordplay, hence my affection for Kochanowski as a Polish Donne or Euripides. But when the opportunity for this anthology of his works arose, and I grappled creatively with the *Threnodies* for the first, extended, time, I was bowled over by their beauty. The *Threnodies* are Kochanowski at his best as a poet, even if they are the record of his very worst experience as a man. They are an exceptional piece in his *oeuvre*, and must be exceptionally foregrounded here.

Jan Kochanowski had more than one child, a fact that is made apparent both by the short epilogue to his greatest work, and references within it to a house seemingly full, but which feels empty, at the sudden disappearance of one of them. Orszula Kochanowska, his daughter, died at the age of two and a half years. Anyone tempted to shrug at this, citing demographics eloquent of the high rate of child mortality in sixteenth-century Europe, need only submerge himself in the nineteen poems of this cycle of laments to recognise the depth of the poet's tragedy. Statistics be damned. A father has lost a daughter, and the *Threnodies* are no exercise in poetic craft, they are the record of a parent's unfathomable grief.

This is the significance of Kochanowski's *Threnodies* as far as the history of European literature is concerned. Following Tadeusz

Sinko, Pietrusiewiczowa and Rytel assert that 'the structure of each threnody closely responds to the bases of the classical epicedium, [...] but from the perspective of lyrical value, they "surpass all Roman lyrical poetry."'[21] While not taking issue with Sinko's words, Charles Zaremba interprets them in a way that underscores the poet's innovative approach to the tradition: indeed, 'we find here the stages of the *epicedium*, but in an order that is causal to say the least: exhortation precedes consolation, and sometimes the same stages are repeated.'[22] The reason for this is simple: Kochanowski is not engaging in a literary exercise here,[23] he is writing out of what might be called, with a pinch of salt, therapeutic need. Up until the appearance of Kochanowski's cycle, the genre of the lament was a formal affair, the poetic métier of a court poet who cares less about the demise of the subject of his threnody, than about pleasing the deceased patron's heir, so as to shore up the chances of his continued employment. Kochanowski's *Threnodies* are not only written for an 'unimportant person' such as a commoner, but an even more unimportant person, a child, and what is even more: a girl! But this is not a poet's voice that we hear in the *Threnodies*, but a father's.[24] And concerning the raw emotion seething in what had been an arid poetic pattern, the prose introduction to the whole gives ample testimony to that. He and she are introduced by name — there can be no mistake that this is not somehow fictive or distant from him, and even if the penultimate line might sound like something formulaic: 'Jan Kochanowski, her unfortunate father, offers these laments written with his tears,' that final cry of pain 'You are gone, my Orszula!' rings true as a spontaneous uprush of grief.

---

21   Pietrusiewiczowa and Rytel, p. 104.

22   Charles Zaremba, 'La disparition d'Ursule: Contribution à l'étude des Thrènes de Jan Kochanowski,' *Revue des Etudes Slaves*, Vol. 74, No. 2/3, Communications de la Délégation française au XIIIe Congrès international des slavistes (2002–2003), p. 508.

23   Pietrusiewiczowa and Rytel do well to point out that 'In the *Threnodies*, for the first time, Kochanowski belittles the motif of poetic fame,' p. 106.

24   For this reason, I find Reuel K. Wilson's statement difficult to understand: 'Kochanowski always (even in the *Laments*, written on the occasion of his daughter's untimely death) maintained a distance between himself and his subject.' See: Wilson, p. 27.

One of the usual ways of looking at the *Threnodies* is as a description of the grieving process, which runs from unbelief, through anger, bargaining, blame, and, at last, resignation, acceptance. There is some justification for this; certainly the depth of feeling, the sense of the poet (no need here to play with words such as 'narrator' or 'lyrical subject') being knocked off balance is underscored by the amplifications in Threnody I: in calling for the aid of 'all' lamenters to help him worthily mourn his little daughter, he repeats words like 'each' and 'every' six times in the first five lines. But it's all no help at all. In the end, 'vain' and 'vanity' repeat five times, in five. The despair of the poet is expressed in the figure of the mother — present in the cycle, but never taking voice — described as a nightingale, helpless before the fierce attack of the serpent plundering her nest, which she must witness, but can do nothing to defend against.

Death, at the start of the cycle, is nothing natural, it is cruel. And here — this is no criticism of any parent who finds him or herself in the incomprehensible position of having lost a little daughter — Kochanowski begins a theme that will run through many of the poems: the theme of selfishness. It's all about him.

This is the theme of the second Threnody, which is built around an artistic paradox. The *Threnodies* are Kochanowski's masterpiece. Like all poets able to objectively assess his own creativity, he was undoubtedly aware of this, and yet — of course — he'd much rather that this exquisite cycle had never been written, than being made to undergo the death of his child, which was the direct cause of it. This sounds like a platitude, but it does hit the very essence of Kochanowski's ontology: he's a father first, a poet second. These lines at the start of the poem:

> Had I the choice to while away my time
> Concocting fairy-tale and nursery rhyme,
> By God! I'd rather sit and rock a cradle
> Like some old wet-nurse, babbling a silly fable,
> To soothe a newborn gently into sleep
> Than write my baby's dirge, and groan, and weep!
>
> (1–6)

provide a context for understanding the strong cry of despair at the end: 'Better she'd not been born!' (27), which, of course, must be understood as 'Better she'd never died.'

Threnodies II and III link up with VIII through the motif of absence. As at the opening of III, 'You hold me then in such contempt, sweet heir?' (1) as if it had been Orszula's choice to depart, there Kochanowski seems to 'blame the victim:'

> You've turned my home into a desert place,
> Orszula, vanishing without a trace!
> So many here — and yet it seems, no one...
> How big the void when one little soul's gone!
>
> (VIII:1–4)

Most interesting here is the image of absence. The whole of her is gone from him, body and soul, 'no trace' of her is left. But is that true? What is he doing here, as we proceed through the *Threnodies*, if not finding traces of her everywhere, almost obsessively so? He does have a full house — besides Hanna, mentioned at the conclusion of the cycle, they had other children too. Five, in fact: Ewa, Poliksena, Elżbieta, Krystyna and Jan. And yet although Orszula's death has created this void, he cannot stop seeing her everywhere. Paradoxically, her physical absence makes her even more present. As he says in II, although he never thought to write lullabies or works for (his) children, taking them for granted, as it were, it is only now, when the good spirit of the house — Orszula — has vanished, that he remembers how full his life was with her there, and regrets all the time he could have spent more consciously with her, while she was.

Better had she not died, of course, but die she did, and this interconnectivity of essence and vocation — grieving father / poet — leads in Threnody III to the first mention of the Orpheus myth, which Kochanowski wields to such powerful effect.

> In such grief am I sunken now!
> Delightful child! Never more to return
> Ever to comfort me, although I yearn,
> And weep, and pray — Nothing to do
> Now, but to set myself to follow you
>
> (8–12)

he cries out in his despair. The classical metaphor of Orpheus, the poet who journeyed alive to the underworld on the strength of his musical talent to plead for the return of his beloved Eurydice, may be an obvious allegory to be mined by a poet who has lost his daughter. But the manner in which Kochanowski develops the allegory in Threnody XIV is striking indeed:

> But if that god has such a heart of stone
> As to be moved not by a father's groan,
> Since I'd have dragged myself all that long way,
> Resigned, I'd sit down at her side, and stay.
>
> (17–20)

In these four concluding lines, Kochanowski hits at the very core of the absurdity of the Orpheus myth. If that poet had truly loved Eurydice so much as to journey to Hell to retrieve her, when he lost her again by his own fault, was his love for her not great enough to have him turn back and remain by her side? To take up residence in Hell before his time, just to remain beside her? *That's what I would do*, Kochanowski says, *if I had the opportunity you had!* And here we see the true humanist spirit at work, which doesn't just toss out a classical allusion, but reinterprets it, suits it to the speaker's own situation. The scathing charge lain at Orpheus' feet — why did you keep walking out into the sunlight, once you realised that you were unsuccessful? — is one of the most effective and convincing manifestations of the depth of the father's grief.

All poetry is communication. As such, there occurs to us the as-yet unasked question: to whom is Kochanowski speaking in composing these poems? At the beginning of the cycle, of course, he directly addresses Orszula herself. Doubtlessly, too, the *Threnodies* are a sort of therapy for both Kochanowski and his wife — a manner of coming to grips with the tragedy by expressing it in words, actively thinking it through. But there is another Receptor, hinted at just after the middle of Threnody IV: 'And she — had only God so willed it! — she / Might yet for many years have gladdened me' (11–12). Kochanowski is not yet shaking his fist at God, but in these lines we see him lifting his eyes heavenward for the first time. Here begins a shift from contextualising his grief in classical tropes toward an almost modern, and risky, one might suggest, personal blaming of the Christian God. At the risk of injecting levity here — far be it! — Kochanowski starts gearing up towards a Jamie Lenman type howl 'This time it's personal!' Now, his return to a classical reference at the very end: comparing himself to Niobe (17–18) might have emerged naturally, even if subconsciously, from his Christian mind's horror at his daring to challenge the Almighty, even subtly. For 1) if one can say that in the context of the myth, Niobe deserved her punishment for her hubris, 2) what did Kochanowski ever do? How did he ever so offend God, as to move Him to take away his daughter as punishment? This line of thinking is explicitly stated, Job-like, in lines 17–24 of Threnody XVII, where he says:

> And even I, who've led a tame
> Life, modest — no one knew my name —
> And neither spite nor jealousy
> Had any cause to bother me,
>
> Smote by the Lord, Who never balks
> To pound the sorest spot, Who mocks
> All prudence, salts my wound the more,
> For striking when I felt secure.

No answer is given, but the fact that he asks it, comparing himself, in the poem under our present consideration, not to the tested, upright Job, but to the Greek mother in her overweening pride, hints that, just maybe, God had a reason for having done so. Has he taken her from me because I've set myself above Him in pride? Of course, this is a question, not a statement. But here we see the poet, in his despair, flailing about for some way to make sense out of what he's been made to endure. If this is a grieving process, we're still in the dumbstruck, uncomprehending phase. The angry blame will come later — as will the reconciliation.

As we move on to Threnody V, we see the poet come out a bit more daringly in anger. In this poem, Orszula, taken prematurely in death, is depicted as a tender olive sapling:

> Yet should the gardener, clearing weed and thorn
> Hack carelessly, the sprig, untimely torn,
> Will faint away, ebbed all her fragile force,
> To lie at her mother's feet, a tiny corpse.

(5–8)

The image is strong, novel, and effective. But even more than it, in the context of the father's grief, is the image of the 'gardener.' Now, it is not only the classical tradition, but the biblical tradition too, that has informed Kochanowski. And no one from our culture can read a poem describing a garden without, on some level, thinking of *the* garden, i.e. Eden. If so, who was the gardener there? God Himself? And therefore, the Job-like trope begun in IV continues here, with God — at least for now — reduced in Kochanowski's mind to Death, who sends perverse 'fatal showers' of gall upon the earth, withering young sprouts, not nourishing them and helping them to grow.

This is anger. We said before that, on one level, the *Threnodies* of Jan Kochanowski are more about him than about Orszula, more concerned with the torment that he is undergoing now than any pain of hers, although, any observer considering the issue from the side, whether he be Christian or atheist, would suggest that, after all, she can be feeling no pain any more. Still, within this context, it is interesting to consider Threnody VII.

In this poem, the ambit of his grief continues to widen, as Kocha- nowski imagines that even inanimate objects, which had been inti- mate with Orszula — the clothes that touched her body — lament, as if orphaned at her passing. But such is his grief, so does it obsess him, that he is blinded to the other side of the coin, so to speak, in the Christian understanding of death. Note what he says in lines 16–18:

> your father's tamped dirt
> Above your head, burying the hope-chest
> In which all his hopes rest!

These lines can be read as 'all of my hopes are buried now, and gone,' which is certainly the primary meaning. But, hidden within these lines is something hopeful, too. They can be just as easily parsed as: 'all of my hopes are to be found here, i.e. the hope of resurrection that is prom- ised to her as well as to me.' As the Lord says in John 12:24–25: 'Amen, amen I say to you, unless the grain of wheat falling into the ground die, itself remaineth alone. But if it die, it bringeth forth much fruit.' Three centuries later and a few hundred kilometres to the north-west, Gerard Manley Hopkins will 'hide' the same message in his 'Spring and Fall,' the point of which is that we *must* die in this world, otherwise we will never

CHARLES S. KRASZEWSKI

be born anew into the life beyond the grave that will never end. In these lines Kochanowski is setting himself up, as narrator, for the lesson he will learn later, when he finally becomes reconciled to fate: Orszula's race has been run; she now has her reward. He, on the other hand, is still struggling towards the goal-line, and over-indulgence in sorrow, self-pity, or whatever it is that blinds him to the Christian promise may lead him to catastrophe.

In Threnody VI, Kochanowski seems to take sudden cognisance of the wider world. As if he were suddenly aware of us present in his room observing his private grief, he draws our attention to *our own loss* suffered at the death of his daughter by introducing the 'Slavic Sappho' motif. Although, obviously, it is the parents of the dead girl who are primarily struck with great sorrow at her passing, all of us who love poetry should also lament the passing of this precocious child, who was due to become a great poet herself in future years. In lines 5–6 'From dawn to setting sun / You sang, and sang — and never held your tongue!' Kochanowski gives us our first look at what his daily home-life was like, as long as Orszula was alive, and he also has her speak:

> 'No longer, Mother dear, will I be able
> To help you — set no place for me at table;
> I must give back the keys to this my home,
> Bid my parents good-bye, and go, alone...'
> (15–18)

These lines shrewdly prove his point. If these were Orszula's dying words, they are poetic: the little girl uses strong metaphors to describe what's about to happen to her: 'set no place for me at table,' 'I must give back my keys,' which increase the pathos of the situation, rather than speaking plainly, in fear or sorrow, as you would expect a dying child to do.

Three women appear in Kochanowski's *Threnodies*: his daughter Orszula, his wife Dorota, and his mother Anna. Of these three, it is only the second whom we never hear speak. Dorota remains a silent, if strong, witness and fellow mourner. Although Kochanowski frequently includes her in his references to parental suffering, she never takes voice. Speaking of this *Threnody* in her essay on the 'Polish Roots of Jan Kochanowski's Creativity,' Jolanta Krzysztoforska-Doschek draws attention to the anomalous nature of the mother's silence:

Kochanowski may also have culled this threnody from the Polish tradition of expressing laments over the coffin of the deceased, about which Zygmunt Gloger speaks in the *Encyklopedia staropolska* [Old-Polish Encyclopaedia], indicating also their relation to the term żalniki [pre-Christian cemeteries or funereal urns, from the word żal — 'sorrow'...] For example, the mother, keening over the remains of her daughter, in tears retails in a raised voice a list of all the services dutifully provided by the girl to the household during life (Gloger 1958:13).[25]

If Kochanowski was indeed familiar with this ancient tradition, the roles are reversed: here it is the dying girl who 'retails' her services, not the mother. Dorota's silence is all the more remarkable: the poet stands in awe of her heart, too 'strong' to burst, which is especially noteworthy as she never disburdens it in speech. In this way, Kochanowski sets up the character of his wife in contrast to his own. While he rants on, sometimes babbling angry nonsense in his deep grief and whining about what Orszula's death means to him, Dorota is silent — strongly silent, bearing the woe, and accepting it, undoubtedly aided in this by her faith. While Kochanowski's character will eventually make his peace with God, Dorota, implicitly, has already done so.

Arriving at Threnodies IX, X, and XI, we come to the cardinal point of the cycle: the section of the poem that best illustrates Janusz Pelc's description of the book as 'a lyrical cycle concerning the great crisis of world-view of a Renaissance intellectual and poet.'[26] It might also be considered the nadir of Kochanowski's woe, as it is here where he most violently lashes out at the tradition that has created him: the classical, Mediterranean culture of Greece and Rome, and the Judeo-Christian tradition of his Catholic upbringing, neither of which, he finds, are of any help to him when he needs them most. 'Wretched me!' he cries in line 18 of poem IX, for 'wasting all his days' to struggle near Wisdom's 'porch,' only, at the end, to be flung into the depths. This is a rejection of classical stoicism, the broad horizons of philosophical reflection that are supposed to keep one on an even keel despite the winds of despair — or

---

25   Jolanta Krzysztoforska-Doschek, 'Polskie korzenie twórczości Jana Kochanowskiego,' *Wiener Slavistisches Jahrbuch*, Vol. 47 (2001), p. 86.

26   Pelc, p. 71.

euphoria, for that matter. Kochanowski doesn't entirely deny that such a thing may exist, but — perhaps it's such an ideal that it is not for flesh and blood. This will be what he throws at Cicero's feet later, in XVI:

> Golden-tongued Cicero! Why do you sigh?
> Because Mark Antony's made you to fly?
> For the wise, you said, the whole world is a home,
>   Not only petty Rome!
>
> I thought the only thing to fear was shame?
> That the wise should treat good luck and ill the same?
> Yet look — you fling your books down, and hang your head,
>   Because your daughter's dead?
>
> (13–20)

It's easy to speak of the calm serenity with which one must meet grief (as well as joy) as long as one is not grieving; it's easy to comfort others at the loss of a loved one, but when one loses a child oneself, all stoical evenness disappears at a touch and one — 'like all the rest' is tossed from the heights 'into the dung.'

Threnody X is the cardinal verse of the cycle for more than one reason. First, Kochanowski's despair reaches its apogee here: so eager to make sense out of his daughter's death — why such punishment meted to a small sinless child? — he dares implicitly to question the veracity of his Christian faith. Dissatisfied with the usual answers to 'where is she?' — Heaven, Purgatory — he even admits pagan answers into the equation: the classical underworld, metempsychosis, reincarnation... And we note that this poem of confusion comes right after the one dealing with Wisdom, Wisdom acquired at great cost, yet absolutely unable to help him when he most needs it. But it is also cardinal in the sense of his final plea to her:

> Wherever you may be, dear soul,
> Come, in some shard, if never more you whole
> I may embrace, and comfort me, or seem
> To do, in shadow, vision — or empty dream!
>
> (15–18)

For, at the end, she will come to him in some ambiguous, equivocal manner as he seeks here. And her appearance then can certainly be interpreted as a God-sent answer to his grief: she is in Heaven; it is true what you have been taught since you were small; stop whining and accept. But that is to come much later. What is important here is that whether or not Kochanowski has been so knocked off kilter by his woe that he is no longer certain whither the souls of the departed go with the deceased person's last breath, he never doubts in her continued existence somehow, somewhere. It is significant that he never doubts in the continuing existence of the soul after death. This hard kernel of faith, of the most basic sort of faith, is what will eventually allow him to accept the cards he's been dealt, and return to an even-minded and hopeful, though ever sad, place of comfort.

This upward swing after hitting rock-bottom begins here, perhaps, in Threnody XI, although the poem commences with an even deeper fall: in his despair, Kochanowski not only questions Christian truth as in X, or doubts the worth of learning as in IX, here he makes a positive statement, enunciating with certainty 'what he has learned' — and that is not flattering to the Christian worldview. He accepts the pagan Brutus' assertion that there is no sense in being good: 'Virtue is trash!' (1), and — even more shockingly: 'Has piety ever rescued anyone? / Has goodness evil ever overcome?' (3–4). No! he states: goodness and piety have never helped out anyone; there is no plan to this world, punishing evil and rewarding good... The English reader will come across no greater expression of anguished agnosticism until the great poems of pain written by Thomas Hardy some two and a half centuries on, like 'Nature's Questioning' and 'Hap.' It is here that Kochanowski comes closest to blasphemy — see especially line 7 — and the answer to the question posed earlier: for what sin can an innocent child be suffering in Purgatory? resounds thus: there is no such thing as sin, since there is no such thing as virtue; the punishments meted upon us are arbitrary. This is a direct negation of the whole Christian superstructure, a denial of God.

We should say *almost* a denial of God. For the poet never really goes that far; instead of questioning God's existence, or His justice, lines 9–13 attack, once more, man's smugness and his trust in his so fallible powers of reasoning:

> And we, so wise! Our secret's safely kept
> From simple minds, who don't know we're inept;

We plumb God's secrets! See us brashly rise
On flimsy wings into the lower skies,
No farther!

And although there is still an implicit complaint tossed before God as
these lines continue: 'we will never have the riddle explained to us,' the
poem ends with the poet pulling up short, realising, with a shock of
horror, that the problem may not lie with God, but in him. Not only
are his powers of comprehension as weak as any other man's, he is in an
even worse situation, as suffering has debilitated them even more. His
reason is sick: 'Sorrow, such is your might?! For do I find / My comfort
lost, I now must lose my mind?' (15–16).

So, although in XIII he plunges back into despair (the *Threnodies*
do not follow any straight and narrow path of progression; true to the
actual state of a grieving person's mind, I reckon, Kochanowski's mood
and attitude vacillate between assurance and doubt, comfort and woe),
the upswing continues in XII where the catalogue of Orszula's virtues
negate Brutus' earlier anguished cry. Yes, Kochanowski admits, at least
implicitly, there is a sense to virtuous action. Even if it were to lead
nowhere, to any Heaven or eternal reward, still there is something in
those who are left behind that acknowledges a person's goodness and
worth — and that is enough to encourage us, even if the world be arbitrary, to choose virtue over vice, good action over sin.

Is it true, as some say, that despite it all, human beings have never
really changed much since first descending from the trees? Or was Jan
Kochanowski a brilliant thinker, years ahead of his time? Whatever
the truth may be, it is difficult not to hear some very modern echoes
in this sixteenth-century poem, for example: Albert Camus' assertion
that if the world is arbitrary, existence senseless, that is the very best
reason for a person to live a good, moral, sensible life — to impose at
least a bit of sense upon existence. It is for reasons such as this that Jan
Kochanowski's poetry, especially the *Threnodies*, has not lost, nor will
it ever lose, its immediacy.

Threnody XV sees a tentative return to the classical tradition (it too
is readmitted to the poet's graces on the 'upswing') by a contextualising of his sorrow through the myth of Niobe. In retelling that story,
the poet may be inching toward coming to grips with his own non-
exceptionality. Niobe, unlike Job, is a story that provides a reason for

suffering. Whether or not the penalty exceeds the crime, it is true that Niobe is being punished by the gods for sinning. Although Kochanowski himself (like Job) questions 'why' this has befallen him, here, again subtly and implicitly, through a reflection on Niobe, he is admitting that there may be some reason for this having happened, even though he cannot fathom it (given the sickness of his already fallible reason); there is no reason why he should *not* be made to undergo such sorrow. In what way is he any better than anyone else? Less a sinner? More 'pure'? This is a theme that will be expanded on in Threnodies XVIII and XIX, as the light of day grows brighter the more this Polish Orpheus emerges from the darknesses of Hell.

And emerge he must, as the last lines of the poem in hand: 'This is no tomb. No corpse lies within on cold shelf. / The tomb is the corpse, the corpse is the tomb itself' (33–34) are not only to be read as an expression of sympathy for the suffering mother, but a realisation of the absurdity of the life-in-death / death-in-life imposed upon the sufferer by over-indulgence in sorrow. 'Man's not made of stone,' Kochanowski will state in line 29 of the next lament, which both sounds like a plea to God or fate: 'Human flesh can't bear suffering like this!' and a realisation of how he is *different* from that petrified woman on Sipylus' summit: life must go on. And it is only continued life that can help him regain his composure, as stated in lines 33–36 of Threnody XVI, which contain the first plea of the poet that has a chance of being answered:

> O Time, Father, who wipes clean Memory's table,
> Do that what neither wiseman nor saint is able
> To: heal this heart, take this sorrow dread
> And knock it from my head!

These lines hit the reader with a freshness that is palpable, yet difficult to describe. In short, it is the beginning of letting go. It is somewhat like that scene from Robert Bolt's *The Mission* in which the soldier, who had been lugging his armour behind him in penitence for having killed his own brother in a fit of jealousy, finally has the rope hacked in two by the Jesuit he is accompanying up a waterfall, and the burden of self-imposed guilt tumbles away into the waters far below. Kochanowski has been over-thinking his situation in trying to understand it; just before these concluding lines he cries out: 'O,

CHARLES S. KRASZEWSKI

God-damned Fortune! Matters it at all / From whence the missiles fall?' (31–32) which signals an end to his fruitless search for reason and opens the door to acceptance, humility, and the comfort that can only come from God.

'God alone can end my pain,' he states in line 52 of Threnody XVII. Still, before he can arrive at this confession, which is the last line of the first poem in the cycle that authentically turns toward God, he must still struggle against a perceived injustice. With its shortened line and basically falling rhythm, Threnody XVII savours strongly of the penitential Holy Week dirges like Iacopono da Todi's 'Stabat mater,' and Tommaso da Celano's 'Dies irae.' This is significant, yet before Kochanowski, still 'irate' in his grief, arrives at that final sigh of despairing hope cited above, he must — as Job or Jeremiah — still fling away from him the bitter gall of his resentment, whether justified or not. In lines 21–24 he describes himself as:

> Smote by the Lord, Who never balks
> To pound the sorest spot, Who mocks
> All prudence, salts my wound the more,
> For striking when I felt secure.

Still, when one considers these lines in the context of the Christian theology of suffering, one finds in them less a complaint against God than a statement of fact, a monitory reminder to those who read them. They have a ritual feel to them not entirely different from the painful words of Christ on the Cross: 'my God, my God, why hast Thou forsaken me?'[27]

For Kochanowski himself, the breakthrough comes in Threnody XVIII:

> Unruly children are we Lord, to Thee.
>   In times of blest felicity
>   We give Thee no mind, out of sight,
> The while we wallow in common delight,
>   (1–4)

Compare these lines with lines 5–8 of XVI:

---

27   Matthew 27:46; Mark 15:34.

Our coffers full, it's poverty we praise.
We shrug at mourning on our carefree days.
As long as Clotho's spooling a fair breadth
    Of wool, we laugh at death.

They both speak of man, in the ignorance of felicity, unthreatened by pain, singing through his life like the proverbial grasshopper who never gives even thought theoretical to the onset of winter. But whereas XVI is a bitter description or diagnosis of foolish man's unsubstantiated certainty of the continuation of clear weather, in XVIII Kochanowski castigates him, not for obtuseness, but for impiety. Whether we are satisfied with this or not, here the poet comes closest to giving a reason for his suffering: considering man's sinful nature, no punishment can be said to be 'unmerited.' Thinkers in the Judea-Christian tradition, from St Augustine to Maimonides, would focus our attention on the fact of being brought into a world of original sin, which 'spiritual syphilis' encumbers us with suffering, even though we were not present at the act that injected the bacillus. Sunday Christians should get used to praying to the Lord not only when they're in the foxhole. Of course, in lines 9–12 the poet asserts that even turning to Him when beset by evils or pain is salubrious for men and women who generally ignore Him when times are good. But the important thing here is what he states in the lines that precede those:

Heedless, that all we have comes of Thy grace,
    And vanishes without a trace
    When no return of thanks to Thee
We raise, responding to Thy clemency.
                                        (5–8)

Once again, the poet finally does find a reason for the incomprehensible blow that has fallen upon him. The death of the innocent child can be explained as a punishment. Not a punishment meted to her, but rather to him. God took Orszula because of my own sins, Kochanowski states. How irrational! the reader cries, especially the reader who comes not of the Christian tradition. And that is exactly the point. Kochanowski arrives at the answer he's been searching for not through empirical experiment or philosophical ratiocination; this conclusion is an act of faith. All of the struggles with God and religion that Kochanowski has enunciated throughout the cycle end with his return to the Christian explanations for the presence of evil and sorrow in a world created by an all-good God. This may be dissatisfying to many. The important thing here is that this answer, which Kochanowski struggled with, batted away, and tested for nigh on twenty poems, at last brings him comfort. And one might suggest that, act of faith as it is, it is indeed rational. What's the only thing of which Kochanowski can be certain? He may not be able to say with one hundred percent certainty why children must die; he may not even be able to state with certainty that God exists. And yet independent of the latter issue, a brief look into his own conscience reveals one thing for sure: he himself is a scoundrel. 'How great my sins! I have wrought so much ill!' (25). Even an atheist, who does not think in such terms, if he or she be honest, must admit along with the poet to the commission of a whole range of nasty, unsavoury, evil or (if you prefer) unethical actions, and it is pure human nature, above and beyond any religious tradition, that prompts us to demand a settling of accounts. We've done wrong, and we should make reparations. Christianity didn't invent that. What it did 'invent' is the idea of a merciful Judge who, despite what is due us criminals by the dictates of justice pure and simple, forgives the faults of the penitent in His mercy. And it is just such mercy — not enlightenment — that Kochanowski realises at the end is what he needs, and for which he begs.

'Threnody XIX — or, The Dream' is the only poem in the cycle with a title. It is also the only one that reaches beyond his waking mind. Eighteen laments of conscious spiritual suffering, one lament of comfort via (illusory? real?) spiritual visitation. The ambiguous nature of the experience is constantly underscored. Is it a dream, as the two departed females arrive only after he's fallen asleep after tossing and turning:

> Long through the night I tossed and turned, my woes
> Forbade my spent flesh rest, my eyes to close.
> At last, an hour or so before dawn chased
> The night away, black-winged sleep embraced
> My soul; and at that moment there stepped near
> My bed my mother, with my daughter dear
>
> (1–7)

or after they've roused him from his slumber, and he's conscious again: 'Deeply I sighed, and woke, / Or so it seemed' (15–16).

We've wondered at the *Threnodies* being 'all about me,' but in a certain sense, they are. Kochanowski's first obligation is the cure of his own soul, and here he is warned that mourning, overindulged in, which is bootless beyond the scot of tears owed to the departed (as it can change nothing, and actually, the soul of the dead is in a better place, beyond woe), might lead to an even worse death for the mourner (the second death). As his mother admonishes him:

> harness this mourning, before it raze
> The inner structure of your soul itself,
> Shattering your strength and poisoning your health,
> Just as the flame the knotted wick devours
> When it's left burning hours upon hours.
>
> (22–26)

All of Kochanowski's complaints are proven right, ironically. On earth, joys are fleeting and illusory. Yes, but in Heaven:

> The joys of heaven never fade away —
> True, free of all defect and all decay.
> There is no sickness, nor any worry here,
> While there among you — death, slavery, fear.
>
> (70–73)

Man's wisdom is faulty, beclouded, no help at all; in Heaven true wisdom resides:

> We bask in endless light, live without pause,
> And meditate with joy event and cause;
> We know no setting sun, no darksome night
> Ever deprives us of unclouded sight.
> The Lord Creator, in His majesty
> We contemplate, Whom you still cannot see.
>
> (74–79)

Kochanowski knows, and knew, all this; the problem (the sin he committed?) was that he didn't use it, not as complaint, but as affirmation — now Orszula has passed through to a better state than mine, and I should… rejoice at her victory, not beweep her fate, or mine. Recognising, even before, that He 'cannot see' God, why did he consider himself empowered to pass judgment upon Him and His verdicts? Kochanowski, as prideful as the man he castigates in lines 5–6 of Trifle III.76: 'Man, who's never seen God, yet will profess / Himself framed in His image and likeness?' was acting like a judge who pronounces on a case while remaining in total ignorance of the matter, before any evidence has been produced.

If there is a 'cycle of mourning' that runs its full course in the Laments, it is in lines like these where it is found:

> All
> The tears in the world will no soul recall
> To flesh once liberated, and unjust
> The man who won't submit, as all men must
> To the decrees of fate, deeming at whim
> She may flog others freely — but not him.
>
> (130–135)

They not only castigate Kochanowski for the selfishness of his sorrow — putting the 'ah poor me!' trope into its proper context — but rhyme thematically with the very first of the Laments, that pitiful beggary of tears which, even had he accumulated 'all' the tears of all the world, all of history, still they would be powerless before fate, or God's will, and (as his mother warns him earlier) might only serve a still greater ill: drowning him.

The fact that Orszula does not speak in the dream is of extreme importance. What, the Slavic Sappho, speechless? Exactly. Everything for which Kochanowski valued her during her lifetime: her childish beauty, even her poetic potential, which, as we have seen, he uses to include us in his sense of loss, are shown to belong to this world only, and not to her essence, that of a blessed soul, to whom the writing of sonnets is irrelevant. All earthly things fade: Kochanowski has been lamenting something, someone, who has vanished. She who remains — who still loves and prays for him and his wife in the blessed regions — here too only assumes the appearance his eyes can recognise in order to bring him comfort. Her blessed reality — her true nature, glorified by God — is something he, while still in the brittle flesh, cannot even conceive.

Finally, the cycle ends with the epitaph for Hanna Kochanowska, Orszula's sister, who also died young. This poem is often overlooked by translator and scholar alike as a mere quatrain of courtesy pinned onto the cycle, which they feel is completed with XIX. It's almost as if Kochanowski didn't have the strength or desire to elaborate the cycle once complete. But no, that would be to see the *Threnodies* as exactly what they are not: a mere exercise in mastering a literary genre. Rather, the epitaph shows that Kochanowski has grown by his experience of Orszula's death and the grief into which he was plunged, and has internalised the teaching brought him by his mother: he grieves his loss, but shortly, and wisely — the grieving father no longer beats his head against a brick wall. Spurning the things of earth, he is intent on the 'deathless joys' now tasted by both his little daughters, and his mother, and which await him when he shall rejoin them.

THIS TRANSLATION

is almost entirely new. The English version of *The Dismissal of the Grecian Envoys* was completed as early as 1985, and published by Players Press of Studio City, California, soon thereafter. The text here has been modified slightly, but in one or two cases significantly, in collaboration with James Wallace, who directed the dramatic reading of the *Dismissal* at Shakespeare's Globe Theatre in London in June 2019. One or two of the Songs and Threnodies were also translated in the eighties, but never published. The rest of the texts were freshly translated between 2020 and 2022 with the great and faithful support of my publisher, Glagoslav Publications, and the Polish Book Institute. I also owe a debt of gratitude to Marta de Zuniga and Natalia Puchalska of the Polish Cultural Institute, London, at whose invitation I participated in the unveiling of Andrew Lilley's statue of Jan Kochanowski in Anne Hathaway's garden in June of this year, and who encouraged the translation every step of the way.

I have tried to present Jan Kochanowski to the English reader from several, if not all, of his aspects as a writer. Besides *The Dismissal,* I include a translation of his translation (*sic*) of the opening hundred lines of Euripides' *Alcestis* — what a shame that he didn't finish it — and 'Guesses' (in Polish, 'Wróżki'), a Platonic dialogue that does double service, displaying the poet's light touch in that unusual dramatic form, and revealing, by the way, something of the political thought of this man who was involved in the current events of his homeland. The reader will also find a few other short prose pieces here — chosen for their interest; his work on Polish orthography would make little sense to the non-Polish reader (and isn't of much interest to the Polish reader for that matter, either, unless he be a historical philologist).

Kochanowski is, above all, a poet, and I hope that my translations of his poetry would not make him blush and shake his head. But of course, I cannot be the judge of that. I can say that, in selecting from the *Songs* and the *Trifles*, I was guided, first, by which of the originals struck me, and second, by which of my translations of these poems seemed to 'work' in English. I am sure that there are some rough passages in them, but I hope they are few, and, of course, these are solely to be lain to my account. If there is anything in them that delights, that is due to Kochanowski. As with all my translations, if any of these spark enough interest in the reader to impel him or her toward inspecting the original Polish versions, my efforts will be richly rewarded.

If I needed to sift through the *Songs* and *Trifles* to cull a solid selection of poems that I reckon might strike the English reader with the same force as the originals do the Polish, I had no such difficulty with the *Threnodies* (*Treny*, also called the *Laments* in English). This masterpiece of Kochanowski's, which he would certainly have rather wished never to have written, is solid through and through; my feeble efforts at bringing the entire cycle over into English are included here, as is the full text of *The Satyr, or Wild-Man*, as an example of Kochanowski the narrative poet. I wish there could be more, but that would require a poet 'on his way to Czarnolas.'

17 September 2022
West Springfield, VA

POEMS

Songs

Trifles

Threnodies

The Satyr, or The Wild-Man

SONGS (1586)

selections

I.2

Swells the heart in Springtime's warm embrace!
Not long ago these woods were barren wastes
With snow piled near our elbows; waggon-teams
Creaked safely over the ice-covered streams.

But now each tree has clothed itself anew,
The blossomed meadows brave a brilliant hue,
The ice is thawed, and on the pristine rill
Both barge and skiff new-carved disport at will.

Now from both wold and wood there echo laughs;
The corn breaks soil, coaxed by the western draughts;
The clever birds entwine sturdy abodes
And start to sing before the dawn is old.

Yet no rejoicing surpasses the supreme
Tranquility of him with conscience clean,
Who, searching through his heart no shame there finds
With which to call to fault a reckless mind.

You needn't spill for him the wine's red flood
Nor sing, nor strum on lutes to prop his mood:
With water he might well contented be
For he is drunk on heady liberty.

But he whose heart's tormented by the beast
Of guilty funk relishes no rare feast.
No song will gladden him, no verses move
Whose ears are stoppered fast with self-reproof.

Good thought, whose company no man can lure
Though he have silk-hung walls and golden door,
Contemn not this my shady bower-plot
Though I be sober, or by drink besot.

JAN KOCHANOWSKI

I.5

Whoever has bread
Enough to be fed
On lucre needn't cast an envious eye,
Cares not for village, town, or castle high.

A true lord, God wot!
Happy with what he's got.
Whoever seeks more to puff up his pride
Gives proof that he'll be never satisfied.

The man who would hoard
Serves a fiercer lord
Than he who must pay tribute to the Turk
Or breast incessant Tatar raids. Hard work!

The King of Macedon,
For a brief moment won
The world entire. Yet still he thought it rough
To have so little — one world was not enough!

What are they worth: your realms,
Armed might that overwhelms?
They win the heart of no girl true and fair;
No treasure overcomes one nagging care.

For death — today remote,
Soon grabs all by the throat:
The richest magnate and the meanest slave
Settle accounts outstanding in the grave.

And yet the greedy man
Would snatch all that he can.
Though piling sacks of gold on golden sacks
The fevered miser always thinks he lacks

Something. But soon you'll find
You'll leave it all behind:
Of all you've scrounged through your skimped life bereft;
And who knows to whom it all will be left,

The swung-wide armoured doors
Admitting to your stores
Your boorish heir. And all your choicest wine…
He'll use to rub down horse-flesh till it shine.

I.6

Although your departure, sweet girl, makes me ill,
I would not hold you here against your will.
All happiness go with you. This I pray,
Wherever through the world your steps may stray.

You see yourself what angry winds arise
To pummel the dark clouds across the skies.
I've seen what storms can do when gales rave
And lash relentlessly the salty wave.

Let savage pagan wives and children test
The dangers of the swelling ocean's breast
As wind-whipped billows shatter ship and pier
And make the very cliffs shiver in fear.

Learn from Europa's hard fate, the poor fool
Who thought to lark a short ride on the bull:
No sooner seated on his back, the strand
Vanished from her sight. Far from solid land,

What was the terror she felt, to espy
Nothing on either hand but sea and sky,
Bobbing amidst the plumbless, frothy tide
With no one near — except her devious guide!

At last, when crumpled on the Cretan shore,
With wild hands at her fair locks she tore,
Sobbing: 'O, Father dear! Gentlest and best,
Whom I've abandoned through my recklessness,

'On this far shingle, how may I begin?
One death is meagre penance for such sin!
Am I awake? Or do I merely seem
To sob so? Is this but some guilty dream

'Flickering through deceptive gates of bone,
Strange images to make me weep and groan?
What was it worth to cross the broad-backed sea?
Was it not better, on the spangled lea

'Among the flowers? If only I could get
That bull in these two hands, I'd make him sweat!
The horns would droop upon that shameless steer
For all I ever lately held him dear!

'I had no shame — abandoning my home;
Nor have I now that thus my death postpone.
O God, if Thou heed'st when a wretch entreats
Thy pity — set me naked among beasts!

'Before the mould of age befoul my face,
Depriving this flesh of its charm and grace —
Set wolves to ravage smooth flesh, lap hot blood,
And scatter my young bones about the wood!'

Villainous girl! He presses near, your father —
This fir will bear your weight; or if you'd rather
Smash to the sharp rocks, look: those cliffs are high;
Leap to your death! Surely you wish to die?

Entrust your body to the burly wind
Since you spurn distaff, and decline to spin;
O, royal maiden — soon yourself to fling
Away to pagan mutt — though worth a king.

I.10

Who's lifted me above the clouds, a-wing
To skim and soar gazing on everything,
The whole world spread below me, as I fly
      Through Heaven on high?

Is that the globe of the eternal fires,
The golden sun, which racing, never tires
To pull the seasons through the aether clear
      Year after year?

And there — that disk of changing light I see,
Queen of the stars, and earth's fecundity!
The music of the spheres… A voice, it seems…
      Or are these mere dreams?

Through regions by no fog obscured I sail;
No snow swirls here, nor freezing swarms of hail,
No: around me summer blooms — long, sunlit days,
      Warm, bright always.

Palaces fit for Thy omnipotence
My Lord, virtue's cosmic magnificence
I see with mortal eye, for here reside
      Saints at Thy side!

I recognise you, Lech, Slav, who first gazed
Upon this country in dim, ancient days;
Whose manliness and power led you forth
      To rule the North!

And there sits Krak the king, enthroned on high,
Who on his city trains a loving eye;
Who left to Wanda a strong, wealthy land,
      O, upright man!

Not far from him the clever Przemysł sits,
And he who won the crown by cunning wits,
Swerving past trap and pitfall as his horse
      Did sprightly course.

God abhors falsehood and loves righteousness.
To this the wheelwright Piast bears sure witness,
For he resides in Heaven, who Poland
      Ruled with just hand.

Ziemowit stands to the right of his sire,
Equal to all, but you, Mieszko, stand higher,
Who with Christ's waters of regeneration
      Laved your nation.

And next to him — see, Bolesław the Bold,
Before whom History's scroll lies unrolled,
Like Polish hearts, who, with him for their guide
      Spread far and wide.

Amongst their number stands that great Monk made
King, plucked from his cloister's peaceful shade.
I see the Leszeks twain, and him, though small,
      In boldness tall;

I see Jagiełło, Kazimerzes both,
Sturdy in battle and in keeping troth;
And Władysław — shining like star of gold,
      Crusader bold!

I see that king magnanimous, Olbracht,
With Alexander Zygmunt, he who brought
Poland prosperity, and blessed peace
      When long wars ceased.

O noble spirits! O courageous leaven,
Who bask now in your well-merited Heaven,

Shower us with the grace for which we long,
      And keep us strong!

May he who sits upon your throne today
Rule us in health and good fortune, and may
He rule us long, sober, clement and sage
      To hoary age!

I.11

You shy away from me, Neta untouched,
Like some fawn, to her mother doe so much
Attached, she panics, lost, when from her sight
She strays, and trembles, half fainting with fright

At leaves set rustling by the merest rush
Of wind, or when some lizard in the brush
Snaps with his tiny feet a twig — each sound
Sends her crouching in terror to the ground.

But I'm no savage bear in search of prey,
Or angry lion who your hide would flay!
Stop trotting skittishly behind your dam.
It's time you found yourself a loving man!

I.13

In dark days I invoke thee, O sweet Night:
Upon us, in these woods, pour down thy light,
Who, like a swarm of bees around our sire
Stand watch, until dawn breaks, tending the fire.

Grant him a safe road home O God, be kind —
Crown with success the plans he bears in mind,
Our pious lord, than whom our Polish land
Never had kinder, since her age began.

But now we're plagued by that pagan severe,
Who recently cringed at our feet in fear?
When Starodub was blown unto the skies,
Its crew then made to pay so cruel a price?

When pride abased was by humility
And bloody Dnieper carried to the sea
A horrid cargo, strewing on the shore
Of islands Moscow's wealth, torn heads, and gore?

Dear God! Are we of such fathers — stout, brave —
Degenerate spawn? Spinning in their grave
They must be! Sacred peace! Thou hast one vice:
With thee, brawn turns to flab, and in a trice!

We've more silver today, of gold we've hoards;
Beneath ever more sweetmeats groan our boards;
So what? We banquet on spring ice so thin
One hefty stomp will send us plunging in!

I.14

See how the mountain-tops with snow turn white!
    The northern winds shriek,
    Freezing lake and creek,
The cranes, sensing cold winter's breath, take flight.

And what can we do, in thicker wraps dressed
    But lay on fresh cords
    Of wood, and on our boards
Set wine — and let God deal with all the rest!

What's in the offing we shall never learn.
    Don't beat your pate, or
    Fret: *What comes later?*
Fate's in God's hands to prop, or overturn.

Hopes distant our short span impatiently
    Bears. Use what's at hand,
    And catch as catch can:
What's to come, that no one can guarantee.

Old stags new antlers sprout between grey ears;
    When once we vigour lack
    Our youth never comes back.
We haven't yet seen the worst of our years.

I.15

'Tis through no fault of mine — for all I know —
That you are so determined, dear, to go;
Search as you wish. No reason you'll descry...
Perhaps some other man has caught your eye.

I won't oppose you. What more can I say?
I only wonder at the curious way
Of women — so unstable! With each wind
Like well-greased weathercocks, one sees them spin.

There were such times... Now, I'd say, days of old,
When I amongst men fortunate was told;
When I had everything, having your love,
And dwelt, on earth, as if in Heaven above.

But now, against the bitterest blasts I grope
Blind, having lost all, as I lost my hope.
I know not whence this sudden tempest burst,
With what foul witch's treason I've been cursed.

You part from me. I wish you well. Be blessed
Wherever, with whomever your heart rest.
But recognise in me a true friend, kind,
The sort, my love, it's very hard to find.

Place not your trust in smooth cheeks, fondling hands —
That were to build your house on shifting sands.
The sun that shines at dawn at dusk will set,
And as the wrinkles grow, so does regret.

You'll age, decline, you blink, and... have you died?
With so few to lament at your graveside?
Ah, such a friend I wished to be for you,
Except that your tears should my grave bedew.

I.21

You sleep; while here outside I busk
Through the long night, to dawn from dusk,
My bones pierced with the chill of night...
Have mercy on my wretched plight!

Just listen how the fierce sleet falls,
Battering roof and drumming walls!
Wake up! And sweeten my distress
With one word, woman pitiless!

No brigand I, although I stalk
Your pebbled pathways after dark;
But what you'll give, I'll not forsake it;
As for the rest, the devil take it!

You'll never find a bolder heart
Than that which suffers passion's smart.
Smooth cheeks make the stunned bend the knee,
But love grows with gentility.

Are you listening to what I say?
Does my voice not reach you where you lay
Your pretty head? Then hear my groans
Ye shades of night, ye tongueless stones!

Ye woods, who to the lyre swarmed
Of Amphion, by his music charmed,
And all of you enchanted rocks
That formed walls as if well-dressed blocks,

And all ye beasts, who wept simoons
When Orpheus twanged his mournful tunes,
Heartbroken, sunk in deepest woe
Seeking his wife who'd fled below,

Whose mournful songs, against all odds
Moved even iron-hearted gods
To let her breathe once more sweet air;
Yes! Had he taken better care

He would have won her back! But no —
He hastened to a deeper woe,
He glanced behind and Hell's harsh law,
Swept her back down with ruthless claw.

But I don't blame him. Where there's great
Desire, it's bloody hard to wait!
Patience — harsh discipline, it's clear,
An hour to lovers seems a year.

How long must I strum these my strings?
Listen — the monk for matins rings!
The world runs backwards. Here I keep
Vigil — refreshed, they rise from sleep!

Good night, then. Thus I here bequeath
To this wet branch a lover's wreath.
Here let it dry in the dawn's light
A witness to my sleepless night.

II.2

I care not if the stones, perchance,
To my plucked melodies should dance;
No wolves need listen to my song;
Ye forests: stay where you belong!

Hanna, for you alone I sing.
Give me your love — I've everything.
And thus surpass I Amphion
And that lutenist Arion.

I can't be moved by pretty face
Alone, or ancient, noble race,
With sire and grandsire famed in battle,
And all that parchment-musty twaddle.

I lay all of my verbal arts
Before one girl of cultured parts.
Should these songs but merit your praise,
I'd care not what the critic brays!

Virtue must bear with jealousies
Like winds that flog the noblest trees.
But we, wrapped in each other's arms
Are free, and safe from envy's harms.

Yes; if my lowly stoop might beg
The presence of your pretty leg,
Ah! What a leg! What do I need
Else? Heaven comes with you, indeed!

These very walls sigh out your name
And groan 'If only Hanna came!'
The linden tree will bend and sway
Hoping to glimpse you on your way…

So have them hitch some horses fleet,
And pack your grip, and take your seat,
And set those steeds to galloping!
The woods are lush with verdant spring,

The fields are spread with blossoms sweet,
The hare finds cover in thick wheat,
The farmer's heart swells, proud and large
Dreaming of grain-encumbered barge,

The flocks are frisking at the pool,
The shepherd, resting in the cool
Shade, pipes his sweet and simple notes
To which the fauns skip (or are they goats?)

Hurry! Before the axle-tree
Of stars sinks in the western sea.
Too soon the shades snuff out the light
To whelm us in unwaking night.

II.5

A shame that to the highest Heavens cries,
O Pole! As unrevenged Podolia lies
Ravaged, beneath the scabrous pagan's boot,
Who on the Dniester's banks divvies his loot!

The faithless Turk let slip his rabid hounds
Who snatch your does amidst their leaps and bounds
And bear them hence — with all your offspring, too —
Far, ah, hopelessly far away from you.

Some sold as slaves, beyond the Danube sent;
Others to Asian hordes, in fetters pent;
And noble daughters (O, Thou mighty God!)
Kennelled in harems Ottoman turn bawd!

By bandits we're raided, by bandits killed,
Who neither city firm nor village build,
But pitch their rugs upon our meadows, where
Us they consume, disordered, unprepared!

Thus on the scattered flocks prey wolves at will,
Fearing no shepherd as they tear and kill;
The shepherd's gone. He's far away from here
And no one leads the valiant sheepdogs near.

If we cannot oppose such flimsy men,
If we so swell their courage, Poles, what then?
They've all but set upon our throne their king —
Consider that! And feel you not the sting?

Come! Rub the sleep from out your gummy eyes
O valiant Lech! Strap armour on, arise!
Who knows on which side victory will be found?
Until Mars tips the scales, stand your ground!

Don't give an inch! Consider well now, see
How best to make him pay, your enemy;
Settling accounts in species: Turkish blood!
To cleanse your shame with its hot, crimson flood.

Shall we to horse? Or are you still at board?
O, wretched feasts, and yet more wretched lord
Who laps from silver plate, while iron Mars
Prepares a second course of bloody wars!

Melt down that silver into coins to pay
The soldiers eager to join in the fray,
Lest their brawn wither, rattling beggar's bowl —
Or care you not, as long as you be whole?

Come! Fund the army! Stand to! Readiness
Is worth a universe in war's distress;
Strap on your plackart now to guard your thew.
It's too late when a pike has run you through!

I like this rhyme: 'A Pole wise, after harm.'
Now, if that cuts close, makes your blood grow warm,
Let this my warning be a better school
Lest, after, and before, you'll be a fool!

II.8

Who'll be our king? O Mikołaj, don't fret:
The writ of his election is now set
Before the throne of God; in adamant
Eternal chiselled by no human hand.

Expect him not at midnight nor midday,
Whether from East or West he'll make his way.
He will be king whom the Lord God selects,
Who to what's just the human heart inflects.

He holds at nought our well-made (futile) plans;
Smiles at our plottings with our neighbour-lands;
Like those which, here, from there, a French prince led…
And had us choose another, when he fled.

Where are those promised heaps of glittering gold?
Those Gascon regiments, armed, stout, and bold?
What for, those tournaments and salvos? Hope
Vanished with them, like pricked bubbles of soap.

It's Fortune shifts the hulls upon the seas;
Fortune, in war, the victory decrees;
'Tis she that rebel, and parliament, heed:
Her choice, men's plans to overthrow, or speed.

Down with all orators and pundits, down!
On some pole in a field let's hang the crown.
If it's not meant to circle brows more wise,
Let it befall him, who more fleetly flies.

II.10

On fields of battle one may win great glory,
In time of peace, by stirring oratory,
But if a man's adorned not by a wife
      Futile is his life.

Of shrewd economy manors are made.
Others amass great wealth through prudent trade.
But with no wife to aid him? Have no fear:
      Watch it disappear.

The honest wife is her man's ornament,
The base which makes his home a monument.
Beneath her rule all things are godly sped,
      She's crown to his head.

She warns of troubles before they draw near
And solves problems as soon as they appear.
With honeyed words she soothes his darkest hour,
      Such is her power.

She bears him a hale brood of girls and boys,
Each like their father, each a font of joys.
No need to search through distant kin for heir:
      He's enough to spare.

Him thricely hast Thou blest Lord, fortunate
In such a union. For an evil mate
Deprives the wretched soul of all he's won
      Ere his life's half done.

II.13

Now lift we to the Lord our praise
In thanks for His abundant grace.
The proud He topples from their chair
And keeps the humble in His care.

That brash, unstinting in his crimes,
Fell tyrant of the northern climes,
Who thinks in this sublunar sphere
Matchless to be, to have no peer,

The Tsar of Moscow — see him yield
To Poland's king the battlefield!
He turns tail, panicked: watch him flee,
Nor will he stop till he's a-sea!

He flies our borders, shuns the towns,
The forts, and all the battlegrounds,
And — (credit's due even to him) —
Succeeds… in saving his own skin.

But hold on, turn your horse back, Tsar!
Let's see how Terrible you are!
You'd have us tremble at your might?
Why then are you shivering with fright?

The time for reckoning's come full soon,
To see who'll doff the cap to whom!
Come, turn the nag, retrace your track…
Who first shall slide off horse's back?

Honour and praise almighty God,
The only King of Poland, broad
And wide, Who boastful despots drags
Down, stifling all their puff and brags,

Who's torn the mask right off the mug
Of Moscow's ruler, brash and smug —
That mask seemed terrible all right,
But look — he's all bark and no bite!

He placed his hope in castles strong,
But these he didn't hold for long;
No one arrived the siege to lift
And all his plans made for short shrift:

Połock he took with might and main
— Before he gave it back again —
Thanks to the hero of this story
The Polish King, Stefan Batory.

Though bullets thick as hail did fly
From deep-set walls and bastions high;
Those iron gates sprung open wide
To let you, Sire, their lord, inside.

Reducing fortress and redoubt,
Castle with crenellations stout,
Still more praise you win, and respect
By holding yourself firm, in check,

Neither raw vengeance nor brute ire
Overmaster you, merciful Sire —
You batter foes to bended knee;
They taste... your magnanimity.

And thus, Hero victorious,
You'll be forever praised of us;
Forever will your poets sing
The glories of their clement king!

II.16

They're nothing worth, your rich delicacies,
Your silver trays, your plate's gold filigrees;
The rose, late-blooming, 's good enough for us!
      Who needs surplus?

For seasoning: mint, that grows most everywhere,
And when a true friend's seated in the chair
Across from you, that's real joy. And to boot:
      When there's a lute!

The lute — proper to dance and learned song;
The lute — comfort to those who overlong
Worry and weep; whose tones soften as well
      The gods of Hell.

II.20

O what a storm you've brewed! What jealousy,
My good bishop, by so abducting me
From home, and leading me so far and wide
From children and a faithful woman's side!

My wife — I can just see her sitting there,
And fuming, that I haven't got a care
Here at your palace: plump, and sleek, and gay,
Served from your stores like my steed on your hay.

Or rather, in uncertainty she'll fret,
Sure that by some disease I lie beset
Which baffles every court physician's art,
And here — so far from her comforting heart!

And then, the household toil, which we should share,
With my absence has fallen to her care;
Alone she house and field oversees,
Feeding our little ones, keeping the peace...

Who knows but that she's withered to a wraith
With worry (though she knows my steadfast faith!)
For there are some who've nibbled delicacies,
Whom later, home-fare never more can please...

And in the grand world there are sirens' songs
Which once hearing, a husband never longs
For wife and children, but would rather stay
Among the brighter set to dance and play.

Such are the worms that gnaw the loving heart
Though true, and hopeful — and that's just the start
Dear bishop! there are more, kind friend, and so —
Be not the cause of (real, or bootless) woe;

Re-join what you have deigned to separate.
'Tis in your power to better the sad state
Of loving hearts, which you apart have forced,
That would not die, as now they live, divorced!

II.24

This quill is no mere feather, Piotr; you
See, I'm a poet, hence, I'm formed of two
Natures, and one that soars. Farewell. Too long
I've bided here amidst the jealous throng,

The cities I contemn. That fellow there
That you call me, for whom you fondly care,
Weep not for him! For he not wholly kicks
The bucket; him the black and foetid Styx

Cannot hold pent. Although he looks a fright,
With sagging flesh, stoop-shouldered, head of white
Like any seagull — ah, but see: there springs
Down on those hands, and from the back grow wings!

With which I shall outstrip bold Icarus
To skim the empty shores of Bosporus
Far-booming; past Surt Cyrene watch me go,
Blest of the Muse, to the far North, where snow

Grips Arctic lands. Muscovite, Tatar, each
Shall know me, and the English too, whose reach
Extends so far; German and Spaniard, yes,
They too, and those who lap at Tiber's breast

To slake their thirst. So, at my funeral
Let there be no keening, or dirge, or pall,
Tapers, or bells, or rich-embroidered bier…
You see, friend, I'll be far away from here.

II.25

What dost Thou ask of us, O Lord, for Thy abundant treasure
Of grace and clemency and love — gifts that surpass all measure?
The Church encompasses Thee not, the world is full of Thee —
Mountain and valley, heaven's heights, the deepest depths of sea.

Of gold Thou hast no need, I know. From pole to torrid zone,
Quite all is Thine, which prideful man would like to call his own.
To Thee, then, let us raise our thanks, with a sincerest heart;
There is no better offering a mere man may impart.

Thou art the Lord of all the world, the vault is thy creation
That stretches wide aloft, embroidered with bright constellations.
'Twas Thou that fixed the massive earth upon its sturdy base,
And with the varicoloured blooms bedecked her blushing face.

The raging Ocean keeps his bounds at his Master's command
And tamely, like a puppy, gambols on the shingled strand;
The rivers surging to the sea first nourish the strong wheat,
And Day and Night wheel rhythmically in alteration meet.

The seasons pass in order: first, the blossoms of the Spring
Arrive before the Summer, laden with the sheaves she brings,
By Autumn followed with her treasures: apples and red wine
With which to cheer the long nights round the hearth in Win-
tertime.

'Tis Thou that sends the dew upon the fainting herbs at night,
'Tis Thou that spills the cooling rain upon the corn parched white.
Thy loving hand spreads fodder fat before each grateful beast:
All flesh and fowl takes nourishment at Thy most glorious feast.

Thus, Lord eternal, to Thee these meagre lines of praise I send:
Thy grace, Thy boundless goodness, and Thy love are without end.
Preserve us, mighty God, as Thou seest fit, amidst the fragile things
Of this world — keep us always safe beneath Thy loving wings!

TRIFLES (1584)

selections

I.3

On Human Life

Nothing but trifles — everything we do.
Each thought and each intention — trifles, too.
There's nothing stable anywhere on earth,
And all your care and prudence — nothing worth.
Honour and beauty, might, money, and fame,
Are like the meadow grass, and fade the same.
We're puppets merely — wretched laughingstocks,
And when the show is over, they toss us in a box.

I.7

On a Mature Woman

She minxes up to me, and flirts. God's truth!
And she already so long in the tooth?
For Pete's sake, no! I turn away in scorn:
The petals dried and fallen, who wants the thorn?

I. 14

Crabs

Love-we the-ladies not ourselves I-advise.
Proven-true-always they-are,-not theirs:-disguise!
There inhabit virtues not vices indeed,
Fair women abound in-prudence not greed.
Creatures such faith not treason they-espy
Features beauteous! where is-found truth not lie.
First-of-all kindness not wealth they-implore,
Thirst they for-love not money they-adore.
Aim I at-fools not,-from-the-heart I speak
Plain-meaning not deception I seek.

I.16

On a Wordy Girl

If no, then no. If yes, good. Let's begin.
My head is splitting from your useless din.

I.18

On One Who Keeps Not Her Word

I thought to get what you would give
(You vowed it 'on your life' — you live…)
But — just like Eve, her every daughter:
Your promises are writ on water.

I.21

On a Pious Girl

If you're so sinless, sweet, tell me, at least
What is it that you whisper to the priest?

I.30

To Jakub

You chide me that my trifles are so small?
Yet yours are smaller, for you've none at all.

I.31

Epitaph for Kos

Weeping, lamenting, Kos, although in vain,
Behold your friends plod in your funeral train,
Who just the other day with you did sit
Quaffing the beer, and trading barb and wit.
But death to all men comes. Trust not good health,
Beauty or youth, to say nothing of wealth.
For when we're called aboard dire Charon's boat
Nor tears nor bribes are worth a single groat.

I.44

On the Holy Father

'Holy' I can't call you. But 'Father?' Yes —
No shame in stating what your sons confess.

I.53
On a Mathematician
The sea he's plumbed, circumferenced the earth,
Plotted the dawns and mapped each planet's birth,
He knows the stars, the Fates, all occult lore...
Yet cannot see that his own wife's a whore.

I.61
On a Lad
Milord once sent the carter out to carry
A certain girl near, secretly; he tarried
So long, Milord was at wit's end with worry
(Been up for hours! The old man's in a hurry...)
He peers through window: 'What's taking so long?'
...And sees them there! At it, hammer and tongs!
'You got it backward, son, upon my honour!
I told you *carry her* — you're riding on her!'

I.79
On a Spanish Doctor
'Our doctor says he's going up
To bed.' 'What? He won't deign to sup
With us?' 'No fear. Pay him no mind.
We'll see him later. Now it's time
To feast!' They ate, then 'Let's go up
To Doc!' 'Yes, let's! But take that cup!'
'Sweet doctor, it's your friends! Knock, knock!'
(He stirs not, but the door's unlocked...)
'God grant you health! Here: Bottoms up!'
'I really...' 'No harm in one cup!'
One leads to two, and two to nine:
Soon the good doctor's feeling fine.
'Strange are the doings in this house:
You lie down sober, wake up soused!'

I.88

To Love

Fervently, I beg you, fierce Love, touch not my heart!
But have your way with any other body part.

I.90

At a Feast

Toilet fee: shilling. Eggs are all my meat!
It's odd when it costs more to shit than eat.

I.95

On Mr Ślasa

Mr Ślasa, turn towards the sun a while.
I'd know the time, yet here is no sun-dial;
For your long schnozzle, gnomon-like, will throw
The hour upon your teeth, as the shades grow.

II.6

On my Linden Tree

Good traveller, rest you beneath my green leaves.
Here sun's heat bakes no one, sun's glare no eye grieves
Though he reaches the zenith and causes the shade
To escape beneath tree-boughs from out the scorched glade.
Here will you be soothed as the cool breezes blow;
Here starlings and nightingales pipe soft and low.
From my blossoms the bumblebee draws his rich hoards
Which as honey and mead will grace gentlemen's boards.
And I with soft whispers ken well the sweet art
To becalm fatigued minds and deep slumber impart.
It's true: I'll bear you no apples, and yet some men hold me
The most fruitful of any Hesperidian tree.

II.19

On a Priest

The Queen would hear Mass — but could find no priest.
At the inn he was, besotted as a beast.
At last, he comes, vested, with wobbly tread,
And she: 'Ah, Father! Long you've lain abed!'
'Sleep? Not me! All were snoring in the palace,
While I was keeping vigil with my chalice.'

II.30

The Gift

Lais gives Pafia her mirror. Does
She wish to see no longer what she was?

II.32

From the Greek

Beautiful Timas lies here on this bed
Of stone, by Pluto snatched ere she were wed.
Now, on her grave-mound, we, her mournful peers
Leave tribute of shorn locks, and endless tears.

II.70

The Gravestone of a Drunkard Woman

'Whose grave is this?' 'Bottoms up!' 'Whose — this tomb?'
'First spill a nice libation — I've got room
For two jugs!' 'Hear me!' 'Pour me a drink, first!'
'I won't drink to you, hag!' 'So much the worse!'
'Tell me your name.' 'The devil take you, knave!
What care you who lies in this or that grave?'
'Farewell, then!' 'What? No beer? And off you fly?
All my life long I've never been this dry!'

II.81
On Thoughtless Rhymes
Only an ass seeks handy rhymes for 'love.'
Bray on, lovers and bards. See the above.

II.95
On Rome
As every nation bowed before the right
Of Rome to rule — as long as she had might —
So now, tripped up, she shivers and she frets,
Perceiving on all sides new mortal threats.
Much better fares her tongue, which men still praise;
Ash yields spear-shafts; the best fruit — comes from bays.

III.25
From the Greek
Down from their pastures the herds come shambling in
Back to their byres, alone, with rain-slick skin.
Poor herdsman Tirimachus sleeps the long
Sleep, pierced by the lightning bolt's trident-prong.

III.27
On Hector and Ajax
Hector gives Ajax a fine blade;
Ajax a belt in friendly trade
Gives Hector. Then, Achilles drags
Hector, that belt hitched to his nags,
While Ajax, glum with wounded pride,
With that sword commits suicide.
The moral's not that hard to sift:
Beware the friend that bears a gift.

III.56
On a Priest
The priest ordained must have no wife, the law
Demands, nor may his members have a flaw.
Tonsure him not then, leave his hair where it falls:
Far better 'twould be to snip off both his balls.

III.76
Man Is God's Plaything
A truth so plain as to make Homer nod:
The fact that man is the plaything of God.
For what's man ever done, from the very first,
That's not made God laugh till His sides would burst?
Man, who's never seen God, yet will profess
Himself framed in His image and likeness?
So blind and so conceited, he's this whim
That the whole universe was made for him!
Man was, and is, and always will be. The rule:
Where the King is, you'll also find the fool.

III.78
A Riddle
There is a beast with but one eye
That always in its crotch doth lie;
Sleek, hard, and heavy are its rounds —
It belches: you'd think thunder sounds,
And, foh! from that hole, what a stink!
(A gun. Why, what else did you think?)

III.82
To a Girl
Don't run away from me, O maiden fair!
Next to your ruddy cheeks my silver hair
Fits perfectly: as every child knows:
The lily's always wreathed beside the rose.

Don't run away from me, O maiden fair!
My heart's not old, although I've silver hair;

Although I've silver hair, I'm still quite hale:
Garlic has a white head, yet a green tail.

Don't run away, my sweet! Mind the old cat:
With passing years his tail grows harder yet.
The oak tree, though half-dry, with leaves of brown,
Still stands supremely, for his root is sound.

THRENODIES (1583)

Tales sunt hominum mentes, quali pater ipse
Juppiter auctiferas lustravit lumine terras.[28]

To Orszula Kochanowska
gracious, sweet, extraordinary child
who, having displayed all maidenly virtues
and graces in the bud, suddenly,
without warning, at such a tender age,
to her parents' great and unbearable sadness,
passed away — Jan Kochanowski,
her unfortunate father, offers these laments
written with his tears.
You are gone, my Orszula!

---

28   Such are the minds of men, as the father himself / Jupiter enlightens the
burgeoning lands (Cicero).

Threnody I

Each tear that Heraclitus ever shed,
Each dirge Simonides sobbed for the dead,
Each woe, all wringing hands, and every care,
Every pain you can find anywhere,
Each sadness palpitating in the world,
Bring to my home and help me mourn my girl,
My daughter torn from me by impious death —
All my joys vanished with her final breath.
Just so the dragon, scenting covert nest
Slinks near with greedy maw, on slimy breast
To snatch the chicks, the while the nightingale,
Helpless, sends up an anguished mother's wail;
The poor thing hops, and battles, in panicked strife —
In vain, hardly escaping with her life.
'In vain you weep,' you'll say to me in pain.
But — good Lord, what in this world isn't vain?
Vain! All is vanity! Strive as one can,
We're gripped in pincers. Vain the age of man!
What's better, then? Mournful serenity,
Or rage against cruel, futile destiny?

Threnody II

Had I the choice to while away my time
Concocting fairy-tale and nursery rhyme,
By God! I'd rather sit and rock a cradle
Like some old wet-nurse, babbling a silly fable,
To soothe a newborn gently into sleep
Than write my baby's dirge, and groan, and weep!
For such vain trifles I'd derive more use
Than from laments — if only I could choose! —
Cursing Persephone here at the tomb
Of my daughter, stolen from me so soon...
I had no say in it. Other tasks urged,
And now, instead of prattle, I write a dirge!
Like sailor prudent, skimming on the surge,
Avoiding hazards seen — torn on submerged.
Who knows what good may come of these laments
I write, or if there's even any sense.
I sang not to her living; now these groans
I offer to her, dead, and feel my bones
Wither, like hers, in death — O, vanity!
We sing, or sob, by chance! Humanity
Is subject to the cruellest laws — O, severe
Queen of the dead, implacable! O, hear —
My Orszula was still a little girl!
Who decided that she was not for this world?
Hardly familiar with the fresh sunlight
She now must stumble through eternal night?
Better she'd not been born! A few scant breaths,
A couple years, and Quick, quick! Off to death!
Instead of the delight which we were due,
She's left her parents to grieve, to moan, and rue?

Threnody III

You hold me then in such contempt, sweet heir,
Deeming your father's portion much too bare
To suit you? Dear, you're right. Not this whole earth
Can match the slightest sliver of your worth —
Your wit precocious, and your charming mien,
Sure harbingers of what you would have been
Had you lived! Ah, your words, your grace, your bow
Polite! In such grief am I sunken now!
Delightful child! Never more to return
Ever to comfort me, although I yearn,
And weep, and pray — Nothing to do
Now, but to set myself to follow you.
And when we meet there, O my child, please, race
And fling yourself into your Dad's embrace!

Threnody IV

Impious Death! You rape a father's eyes
To make him look on, while his daughter dies!
I watched you strip our tree of unripe fruit
And tear our parents' hearts out by the root.
No matter when she'd die, the same result
You'd gain — it would be no less difficult
For me to bear: in the same sorrow hurled
I'd be, to see her go, in this void world
Leaving me, but that's just to say I burn
With no less woe now, nor might greater yearn,
And she — had only God so willed it! — she
Might yet for many years have gladdened me,
Whilst I, in peace, watching the seasons roll,
Readied myself to render up my soul
To dread Persephone, with no sorrow,
The likes of which obliterate tomorrow;
Now, like Niobe, gazing on her own
Children slaughtered, I weep, and turn to stone.

Threnody V

An olive sapling, in a garden glade,
Will rise toward heaven screened by her mother's shade,
A slender upshoot, climbing from the earth,
Though neither leaf nor branch yet pushing forth.
Yet should the gardener, clearing weed and thorn
Hack carelessly, the sprig, untimely torn,
Will faint away, ebbed all her fragile force,
To lie at her mother's feet, a tiny corpse.
This, Orszula my darling, was thy fate.
Blooming before thy parents' eyes, of late
Just pushing through the soil, Death's bitter gall
Rained down in fatal showers, and caused thee fall
Dead at thy parents' feet. Persephone!
And will my tears not call her back to me?

Threnody VI

My little singer! Sappho of Slavic song,
To whom not only my wealth should belong
In dowery, but my lute, too, had been willed.
Ah, girl: so young, and already so skilled
In crafting song! From dawn to setting sun
You sang, and sang — and never held your tongue!
Just like a tiny nightingale, who fills
The greenwood all night long with scales and trills —
Too soon grown mute! Never more to be heard:
Fierce Death has chased away my darling bird
Before you'd surfeited with song these ears,
And now I pay the chit with endless tears!
You even sang, my child, with your last breath,
Whispering to your Mama at your death:
'No longer, Mother dear, will I be able
To help you — set no place for me at table;
I must give back the keys to this my home,
Bid my parents good-bye, and go, alone...'
Enough! Your father's sorrow chokes him. For
Remembering this, I can recall no more;
Your Mama's heart — O, how it must be strong
To beat still, unburst, at your final song!

Threnody VII

O miserable raiments, you sad gear
      Of my daughter most dear!
Such mournful eyes you seem to train on me,
      Compounding my misery!
No more by those sweet limbs will you be worn:
      She's left us all forlorn!
An iron slumber grips her now, endless,
      And you, bright summer dress,
You, ribbons, golden bands, and pretty shifts —
      Her mother's futile gifts —
Not to this bed, dear, but to another
      Was your poor, poor mother
To lead you, blushing! No such nightgown, no,
      Were her hands to sew!
You've a rough winding-sheet for a nightshirt,
      And your father's tamped dirt
Above your head, burying the hope-chest
      In which all his hopes rest!

Threnody VIII

You've turned my home into a desert place,
Orszula, vanishing without a trace!
So many here — and yet it seems, no one...
How big the void when one little soul's gone!
You — ever chattering, ever humming tunes,
Always underfoot — in all of the rooms;
You soothed your frazzled Mama with a touch,
Nor ever let Dad worry overmuch;
Always there, ready with eager embrace,
Always laughing, always that smiling face...
Now all is dumb. It's like a desert here:
You've no more japes; you've no one now to cheer.
All through the sad house — empty just the same.
The cold heart searches for your warmth in vain.

Threnody IX

For You, Wisdom, one would give all his treasure —
If, truly, you were wealth beyond all measure;
Able all care and worry to uproot,
Making of men angels, who no tribute
To terrors pay, beneath no fate so abject
That as mere passing trifles can't be recked;
On even keel, whether it's happiness
That meets him, or sorrow, or grave distress.
Always unmoved, fearing no mortal doom,
Safe, immutable, ever unconsumed,
You judge good fortune not by coin or station,
But by satisfaction, in meet moderation.
You look with eye unmoved upon the wretch
Who pines in worry, though his roof be thatched
With spun gold; nor will you disdain to be
Beside him thrashed with greatest poverty
As long as he Your sage advice obeys.
Ha! Wretched me! Who've wasted all my days
In toil and sweat struggling near your porch!
Climbing your endless ladder, with your torch
At my fingertips, at the topmost rung —
To be hurled among the rest into the dung!

JAN KOCHANOWSKI

Threnody X

Orszula, my sweet girl, where have you gone?
To what world's region do you now belong?
Have you pierced those clouds, soaring ever higher
To take your place in some angelic choir?
Is it Heaven? Or the Islands of the Blest
Where you abide? Or across the waves funeste
Of Styx did Charon ferry you, Lethe
To sip, and thus forget heartsick me?
Or have you shed your girlish form, to sail
The soft winds, trilling, clad in nightingale?
Perhaps in Purgatory you remain
Until you're cleansed of every trifling stain
Of sin — if you committed any! — Or
Have you returned there, where you were before
Your birth? Wherever you may be, dear soul,
Come, in some shard, if never more you whole
I may embrace, and comfort me, or seem
To do, in shadow, vision — or empty dream!

Threnody XI

Virtue is trash! despairing Brutus cried —
Wherever you glance, rubbish on every side!
Has piety ever rescued anyone?
Has goodness evil ever overcome?
We're pawns in some foe's arbitrary game.
Whether we're good or bad it's all the same:
Where it lists, there blows his pestilent breath —
Both crooked and upright blasting to death.
And we, so wise! Our secret's safely kept
From simple minds, who don't know we're inept;
We plumb God's secrets! See us brashly rise
On flimsy wings into the lower skies,
No farther! All our wisdom — empty dreams
We'll never live to see explained, it seems.
Sorrow, such is your might?! For do I find
My comfort lost, I now must lose my mind?

Threnody XII

No father ever loved a child more;
No heart was ever quite so crushed before;
But then no child had ever seen the light
Who so deserved her parents' love. Delight
Incarnate! Sweet, obedient, and sage,
Who sang, and rhymed, like others thrice her age;
Quick to learn manners, so polite, and mild:
A little lady and a playful child.
Unspoiled and even-tempered, never shrill,
Modest, attentive to her parents' will,
She never sulked. She always took great care
To raise aloft morning and evening prayer,
Greeting her mother ere she went to sleep
And begging God her parents safe to keep.
Sensing her Dad's approach, she'd leave off play
And rush outside to meet him on the way.
Ever cheery for chores, at every task
Eager to help, not waiting to be asked —
All this, at such a young age! Truth be told,
She was no more than, what? — Thirty months old!
So thickly burgeoning with splendid fruit,
Her overburdened stalk snapped at the root
Long before harvest-time. Barely pushed forth,
Such seed I must resow in the black earth?
Yet never more will these my flooding eyes
Behold a green shoot from that soil arise.

Threnody XIII

Orszula! From these arms untimely torn —
I wish… I wish you never had been born!
Such meagre joys paid for with grief immense,
And all because of your departing hence
So swiftly, like some tantalising dream
Of riches — that leaves nothing but the gleam
Upon waking, and deep regret, and yearning…
Just so you tricked me, coming and returning
Into thin air. Now, how am I to cope,
Left here behind, with heart emptied of hope?
When — so unlooked for, girl! — away you stole
From me, taking with you half of my soul?
Stonemasons, here! Bring chisel, maul, and bit —
Here is the stone. And what you'll carve on it:
'Orszula Kochanowska lies below,
Her father's love. Or rather, grief and woe.'
O, stupid Death! You got it backwards! See?
I was not to bewail her, but she, me!

Threnody XIV

Where is that dire threshold that, long ago,
Orpheus crossed, when led there by his woe?
If only I could follow my dear daughter's
Footsteps there, and cross the sable waters
On the stern boatman's skiff, who punts the shades
Unto the far bank with its cypress glades
Gloomy, I'd go! And I would take you there,
My lute — unto the lugubrious lair
Of savage Pluto, whom we'd knead with song
Into one sobbing mass, however long
It took, until, worn down, he would agree
To give my sweetest child back to me,
To soothe at last this pain that wears me thin —
Nor need he fear that she'd be lost to him:
We're all his for the picking, that's for sure —
Still, he should let the fruit swell and mature!
But if that god has such a heart of stone
As to be moved not by a father's groan,
Since I'd have dragged myself all that long way,
Resigned, I'd sit down at her side, and stay.

Threnody XV

O, golden-tressed Erato, and you there, my sweet lute,
Who soothe those whom grief has blasted to the root,
Soothe now my poor tormented mind. I would be healed
Before I become a stone pillar in some field
Pulsing bloody tears in streams through the marble rind —
Of brutal memories and my bleak fate the sign
External — am I wrong? One way to soothe the heart
Is by meditation on others' woe, through art —
Niobe! If we can trust fable, of mothers
Most wretched, compared to you, indeed, who suffers
More? Where is your brood of sons and daughters now, pray?
Where is your delight? Why are you no longer gay?
Seven and seven grave-mounds — fourteen tiny hills,
And you there in their midst, alive despite your will
To die — how you embrace them all, in sorrow wild,
For in each cold hillock, you laid to rest a child!
Just as the pitiless scythe mows down tender, frail
Fieldblooms, just as blossoms battered by savage hail —
What hope is left? What can you expect tomorrow?
Why seek you not in death relief from your sorrow?
Phoebus! Is your quiver empty of swift arrows?
And you, vengeful goddess, why string you not your bows
And — whether out of anger, for she is guilty,
Or, if immortal breasts harbour any pity —
Strike the poor woman down! Ah, but no — cruel, snide,
Your minds invent new torments, heartless! Petrified
By mourning her slaughtered babies, she's turned to stone.
There on Sipylus' summit she remains, alone,
And yet beneath her rough crust, red, fresh wounds endure:
Out gush her heartfelt tears, flowing in streamlets pure
That slake the thirst of bird and beast, while age on age
She's fixed to the cliffside, lashed by the winds that rage...
This is no tomb. No corpse lies within on cold shelf.
The tomb is the corpse, the corpse is the tomb itself.

Threnody XVI

O man misled! O swagger insane!
A trifle, for wit to overcome pain
When fortune smiles, and the world is our thrall
      And we've no pain at all!

Our coffers full, it's poverty we praise.
We shrug at mourning on our carefree days.
As long as Clotho's spooling a fair breadth
      Of wool, we laugh at death.

But when we're thrashed with sorrow or with want,
We find that life's not quite the carefree jaunt;
We only fear death's shadow — when it grows
      Uncomfortably close.

Golden-tongued Cicero! Why do you sigh?
Because Mark Antony's made you to fly?
For the wise, you said, the whole world is a home,
      Not only petty Rome!

I thought the only thing to fear was shame?
That the wise should treat good luck and ill the same?
Yet look — you fling your books down, and hang your head,
      Because your daughter's dead?

You said that death should not be feared by us,
The wise — if that be so, why, virtuous,
When you, for a sharp speech, were to be tried,
      You fled to save your hide?

Your 'sic probos' were fit for all but you.
'Do as I say, rather than as I do.'
O pen angelic! Life's a messy thing,
      And we've both felt its sting.

Man's not made of stone, and as the winds
Of fortune flutter, so his humour spins.
O, God-damned Fortune! Matters it at all
      From whence the missiles fall?

O Time, Father, who wipes clean Memory's table,
Do that what neither wiseman nor saint is able
To: heal this heart, take this sorrow dread
      And knock it from my head!

Threnody XVII

The Lord hath lain His hand on me
Stifling my one felicity.
The soul inside me barely breathes.
Her too, it seems, the Lord would seize.

Whether I watch a new sun rise
Or gaze at sunset, as it dies,
I feel the selfsame searing pain
Of which I'll never be free again.

My eyes are never free of tears,
For they must weep through the long years
Remaining me! Almighty God!
Where might a man escape Thy rod?

Whether we set out on the seas
Or batter our foes to their knees,
At every hand misfortune lies
Although it vary its disguise.

And even I, who've led a tame
Life, modest — no one knew my name —
And neither spite nor jealousy
Had any cause to bother me,

Smote by the Lord, Who never balks
To pound the sorest spot, Who mocks
All prudence, salts my wound the more,
For striking when I felt secure.

My reason, when I still was free,
Raticcinated so gaily.
Today, it hardly functions. Thick
And dimmed, no help to me now, sick.

Sometimes, one would like to forget
One's cares, and smile — while breath is yet
Lent one — but just as I would go
Among gay throngs, I'm checked by woe.

All human proverbs are in vain
That would call by another name
Evil; and he who smiles in grief
Is mad. Insane beyond belief.

And yet they say: Laugh off your tears!
Such rattlings sometimes strike my ears,
But jollity soothes no man's woes.
The pain remains, and greater grows.

For the soul, wounded, must take voice
In sobs and groans — she has no choice.
What brings no honour, taints with shame,
And still the heart's bruised all the same.

Where's the cure for this malady?
As God's my witness — beyond me!
If you could bring this to an end
And quickly, you'd be my best friend.

Until you do, I'll weep and grope
Through shards of life without hope,
My reason flattened beneath the strain —
And God alone can end my pain.

Threnody XVIII

Unruly children are we Lord, to Thee.
      In times of blest felicity
      We give Thee no mind, out of sight,
The while we wallow in common delight,

Heedless, that all we have comes of Thy grace,
      And vanishes without a trace
      When no return of thanks to Thee
We raise, responding to Thy clemency.

Hold fast to our leads, Lord, that we not stray
      After this world's joys, which decay!
      That we, at least, should turn to Thee
In woe, if we wish not to, when carefree!

But, Father, chastise us with loving care.
      For who, dear Lord, Thy wrath might bear?
      This flesh, like snow is soon undone
Beneath the swelter of a brilliant sun.

Eternal Lord, we'd meet a speedy doom
      Should ever Thy mighty hand loom
      Above us in anger. Relent!
Thy displeasure alone is sore torment.

And yet, Thy mercy's known to us of old
      And sooner will the sun grow cold
      Than Thou wilt spurn the humbled heart
Though long from Thee the rebel keep apart.

How great my sins! I have wrought so much ill!
      And yet Thy mercy's greater still —
      Greater than any sin of man.
In pity, Lord, stretch forth to me Thy hand!

Threnody XIX — or, The Dream

Long through the night I tossed and turned, my woes
Forbade my spent flesh rest, my eyes to close.
At last, an hour or so before dawn chased
The night away, black-winged sleep embraced
My soul; and at that moment there stepped near
My bed my mother, with my daughter dear
In her arms — looking as she did when day
Dawned and she'd risen and trotted near to pray —
With tousled curls, in rumpled nightgown white,
Ruddy-cheeked, chuckling in impish delight.
I gasped, astounded. Then my mother spoke:
'You're sleeping, Jan? Or straining at the yoke
Of sadness still?' Deeply I sighed, and woke,
Or so it seemed, and after a short pause
She went on: 'I've come to you because
Of your incessant sobbing, which has pierced
To the land of the departed. Yes, your tears
Have lashed that secret country like flood-water!
On these I've sailed here with your darling daughter
So you might gaze once more upon her face
And harness this mourning, before it raze
The inner structure of your soul itself,
Shattering your strength and poisoning your health,
Just as the flame the knotted wick devours
When it's left burning hours upon hours.
And so — you think we dead are quite undone,
Never more to behold, once set, the sun?
Know then: the more flesh is surpassed by soul,
The more this life surpasses yours. More whole
It is: earth receives earth alone. It dies
Not, the blessed part, the soul, which flies
Back to the heavens whence it came! Don't grieve
At our liberation, but believe!
Your sweetest Orszula lives on — Look! You mourn,
So she appears to you now, in the form
You know — perceptible to your dull eyes.

But know — like the bright morning star, she flies
Amongst the angels now, and all the saints,
And as before, so now, never relents
In prayer for her dear parents, as on each
Day of her mortal pilgrimage, when speech
Was yet a babble of rote, guess, and gist.
Now, have I seen you shake an angry fist
At destiny, for her too-early flight,
Which kept her from this world's meagre delight?
Wretched delights, that disappoint and cloy,
And bring more worry and pain than real joy!
Be your own witness! Do you not complain
That what joy she brought you wilts at the pain
You feel at her departing? You say no?
Good. Savour then the fleet joy, and let go
The rest! God took her at an early age
And, what? He spared her all the shame and rage
That adult life brings — no felicities
Were torn from her, but life's difficulties:
Toil, worry, sorrow; yes, many a tear
Of which the earth's more sodden, year by year.
The bright apple bit smacks of filth and ash;
The wealth heaped up with sweat proves… shiny trash.
What is it you bewail? That she was not
Married? That is to say, vended and bought?
She'll have no husband — is this why you fret? —
To spend her dowry on disdain and threat?
That she's been spared the pains of childbirth
And bitter musing, whether it was worth
Bearing those whom she must lay in the earth
As you did, her? Such are the toothsome sweets
To which this mortal world her children treats!
The joys of heaven never fade away —
True, free of all defect and all decay.
There is no sickness, nor any worry here,
While there among you — death, slavery, fear.
We bask in endless light, live without pause,
And meditate with joy event and cause;

We know no setting sun, no darksome night
Ever deprives us of unclouded sight.
The Lord Creator, in His majesty
We contemplate, Whom you still cannot see.
Thus, change your course, my dear son, in good time,
Preparing for such wealth as in your clime
Cannot be found. You know the joys of earth;
Now, set yourself to strive for things of worth
Incomparable! She chose the better part,
Your girl, like some voyager at the start
Of her embarking, who beholds the sea
Dark, fierce, and turns back to the quay,
While others who unfurled their sails, their skiffs
Are dashed with violence against the cliffs,
Or cast adrift on desert rocks, marooned;
These by the cold, those by starvation doomed.
Life is a shipwreck. How infrequently
One snatches flotsam and escapes the sea
Unbattered! Death was her fate. Will you rage
That she outlived not Sybil in her cage?
She had done with it quickly, mortal life,
Avoiding thus its trouble and its strife.
She's other siblings who remain behind
To be orphaned by you, Jan, in good time;
Another to be hustled out the door
To husband, knowing not whence or wherefore;
Others may be raped — whether by their own,
Or by some pagan bandits made to groan
In shameful service, sobbing with each breath
And suffering a constant, piecemeal death.
Rejoice that your sweet girl's escaped that fate,
At such a tender age passing the gate
That leads to Heaven — where, safely within,
She's free of worry, and the stain of sin.
Her fate was happy, son! O, have no doubt,
And as for mourning her, why, cut it out!
Here on this earth you've one daughter the less —
See that you don't now lose your manliness

JAN KOCHANOWSKI

And dignity, which would be to your cost
A greater perishing than what you've lost.
Now, take yourself in hand. No man is born
Who's not the object of the whips and scorn
Of circumstance, let him strive as he may
To dodge its bolts — they'll strike him anyway.
Willing or not, each man must undergo
The trials of sorrow, and I do not know
Why you should be above the law alone,
Or think it more unjust because you groan.
Your girl was just as mortal as her father —
She lived as long as God willed it — no farther.
Not long, it's true, but it's not up to us,
And who knows if it isn't better thus?
Dark are the ways of God, and our poor wit
Can do no more than keep faith, and submit.
Tears in such measure are unseemly. All
The tears in the world will no soul recall
To flesh once liberated, and unjust
The man who won't submit, as all men must
To the decrees of fate, deeming at whim
She may flog others freely — but not him.
Such are the ways of Fortune, my dear son —
Greet both with placid eye: both lost and won.
We should be thankful, when we've been bereft
Of something, still that something has been left,
For in her power it lay to take it all.
What good is it, against Nature to squall?
Gird fast your heart against the fierce onslaught
Of woe — consider all that you've still got.
Brooding on debit, don't forget the gain.
Speaking of loss, say — was it worth the pain
To educate you? How much wealth it took
To keep you housed and fed, supplied with book
And paper — and for such a lengthy span!
And it was not all swinking, was it, Jan?
Now is the time for gathering the sheaves
Of wisdom — have you not learned how to grieve?

Others you've comforted in their despair,
Now you're beset, and your wisdom's gone... where?
What good is learning that, when time comes round
For application, it just lets you down?
Physician, heal thyself! You have the skill,
And he who contemns healing Time does ill.
Some instant panacea would be great!
But lacking that, patient in wisdom, wait.
Time passes, pain ebbs, and the future brings
Happiness too, that softens bleaker things.
Some we yearn for in anxious expectation
That makes old sorrows lessen in relation.
The whole thing is: past-future, cruel-benign —
Greet all with equanimity of mind.
Bear man's fate like a man. There is one Lord
Of sad chastisement and of blest reward.'
She vanished...I came round... It's still unclear:
Was it a dream? Or were they really here?

Epitaph for Hanna Kochanowska

And you, Hanna, after your sister sped
To visit — too soon! — the lands of the dead.
Leaving your wretched father to lament
All passing joys, on deathless joys intent.

THE SATYR, OR THE WILD-MAN (1563)

TO THE MOST MIGHTY LORD OF THE NORTHERN REGIONS
Zygmunt August, by the Grace of God King of Poland, etc.

My Lord — title most grand among the free —
  Just now I have no gifts worthy of thee,
But, as fat oxen are not always slain
  In wreathéd sacrifice, and incense grains
Speed prayers to God too, deign this work receive
  In such spirit, and clement grant reprieve
To this beast of the forests — a good sort
  If rough — who dares present himself at court.
Of ribald mug (I grant) and antic frame,
  I know not whether he'll be wild or tame
In speech, but thou need'st fear no violence
  Though rail he will at crimes and governments.
Our customs he's not very fain to praise
  And — if he lies not — he since ancient days
Has trod this earth; I finish now — he feels
  I've said enough; he's treading on my heels!

You see me as I am: brow sprouting horns
  Above a phiz uncharming, and I've worn
Such shaggy leggings always. Whether odd
  Or not, in ancient days I was a god
(Or taken for one) — the deep woods my home
  Through which, pensive or puckish, I would roam.
But here in Poland, there's hardly a tree
  You haven't chopped down — so you make me flee
One step before the woodsman. All I see
  Are forests levelled: beech for factory,
Pine to make tar, and oak for the grain-barge;
  I'm banished by man's greed to haunt the marge
Of cave and summit. At this rate, I gauge,
  I'll soon find no refuge for my old age!
Where have I ever seen such rabid greed
  For lucre! Soon they'll have no wood to feed
The hearth in winter. Sure, call me a joker —
  In Poland there's none but merchant and broker.
For cattle sold in Brzeg, who's the most cash?
  To Gdańsk, who's ferried the most grain or ash?
Such are your laurels! While — look to the East:
  There you'll spy Tatars, fiercer than any beast!
Well, times change and men change too; these are facts.
  But there were times wealth wasn't told in sacks
Of coin; it was for churls to till the field;
  True noblemen the knightly sword did wield.
To spend seven years at war was no great thing
  To them, nor hunger's pinch, nor swelter, sting
Of frost… And all their wealth was martial fame,
  Their ornament — worth more than gold — their name.
And when their mind turned to the joys of peace
  That meant not that their martial games would cease;
They never set aside armour or horse
  As if the morrow were to bring new wars.
A standing army was matter of course,
  Nor was their upkeep burdensome to them
Who raised their sons to be not serfs, but men.
  Poland waxed great thanks to men such as these,

JAN KOCHANOWSKI

Stretching her borders till they touched two seas.
   They gave you this Republic, freedom, laws
Of which you are so proud, not without cause.
   And yet — fail not to keep this truth in mind:
Untended realms fall into swift decline.
   Yes, if those days of greatness now are through,
O son degenerate! It's thanks to you!
   You've turned your father's swords to other use:
This one's a ploughshare, that one spits a goose;
   Helmets are hen's nests, or they measure oats
When jarvey raises feedbags to the throat
   Of draught-horse, yes, no steed mettled for battle;
Stable-ox rather, fit for trace, not saddle.
   There's your rittmeister! Who makes peasants skip,
Not soldiers, not with sabre — knotted whip!
   I speak the truth, or not? You judge yourself!
But let none whimper that Poland in wealth
   Hath blossomed due to fieldwork, and, all told,
There's never been here such a store of gold.
   Your fathers had no gold, that's true — but fair
As well it is to say — they didn't care!
   Courage their greatest resource of all things;
By it they laid the law down to rich kings!
   You think it fairy-tale, all winks and smiles
When Kyiv's ambit's set at seven miles?
   Or when you hear of churches roofed in gold
And alabaster buttressed? Yes, of old
   Such was that city. Judge not by present wealth;
Today it's but the shadow of itself.
   It was your fathers' valour and their might
That cast that glorious city from the heights
   Into the depths; of Prussia I will say
Nothing — as you may see yourselves today:
   The thick-set cities and the castles tall,
Roads, bridges, shorelines broad, and armoured all —
   You see yourselves, who sail to Gdańsk each year,
The witnesses to glories past are clear:
   Such splendour comes from great outlay of treasure,

And those landlords had wealth beyond all measure.
   It helped them not, when Poles attacked, for sure!
And those rich men were vanquished by the poor.
   What have you ever done to win men's praise,
You rich? To mention not just ancient days:
   Five times the Tatars wrought their evil works,
Selling your captive brethren to the Turks.
   The Despot, vaunting an usurpéd name,
Twice coursed through here, to your undying shame;
   The Muscovite seized Połock for his throne,
Producing writs that claimed Halicz his own
   (Though in a trial I'd take your side, for he
Is rather dodgy, constitutionally).
   What else? The Swedes stretch arms across the sea
To wrest from your stunned hands the Inflanty;
   And if not for the Wisła, in a trice
Brandenburg would have been here — a steep price
   The Prussians paid to him then! See how bold,
How omnipotent is your pretty gold!
   Tell me — how does it all seem to you now?
Was it worth trading sabre in for plough?
   And that is just prelude to what shall be.
There's more to come, my brothers, wait and see!
   When that brave mask of yours falls from your face
And all the world shall see how far your race
   Has fallen from what your fathers were! Don't trust
To Turkish lethargy. They won't let rust
   Creep on their blades, if there a reason be
To set out for your shores. Is it calm, the sea?
   Now is the time to strengthen your defence.
I'm not sure if the Germans are your friends,
   Or how much trust you place in them; I fear
They've got their eye on you, and every year
   They're creeping closer with their settlements.
But you dig ponds, set palings, not battlements!
   You strip your woods to choke Wisła with naves,
Hacking down forests for potash and staves —
   'Pole comes from *pole*, field,' so they say;

When trouble comes, where will you hide away?
  For those I see here may be good for farms,
But war? Where are your chargers? Where your arms?
  Where is your military exercise,
Sans which the soldier stands not to — he flies?
  So you've grown wealthy. But at such a cost!
Quite all your knightly virtues have been lost,
  Defence not merely of markets and moats,
But of your freedoms and, what's more, your throats.
  Let others study law and settle scores
In courtroom arguments like orators,
  Your wit is good for nothing, soon you'll learn,
Unless your borders be secure and firm.
  You think to overawe your foes with gold?
You only make their appetite more bold!
  But as for me, I hold your wealth at nought,
Though I could wish you'd give it better thought,
  Who, as collateral, villages lose
And all your silverware's pawned to the Jews.
  Shame on the sire with nothing to hand down!
More shame on bankrupts hustled out of town!
  But tell me, for God's sake, how can it be,
With such landholdings you sob poverty?
  It's surplus, neighbours, surplus, like the ocean
Swallowing all, and fostering the notion
  That you're all beggar-poor. It well may be:
There's no more gluttonous lout than luxury,
  That greedy beast! However much you stuff
The maw of wastrelsy, it's never enough;
  All: cattle, peasant… land upon his board
And he devours all — and for dessert: the lord.
  With such a guest as he, the rivalry
Is ruinous: To your toast, he'll raise three;
  Serve fifty courses, he'll claim twice as much —
O, scoundrel courtesy! Whose Midas-touch
  Nicks the poor host of whatever he sets to table;
You're wearing lynx? His collar's warm with sable.
  Your cup is chased with gold? His too — to boot

He's gold upon the slipper on his foot
  (Though sometimes muck, too); he's broader sleeves
Than anybody; his sort never leaves
  The field of fashion without victory —
To keep pace means to rush to penury:
  Than be outshone, why, he would rather die,
And so — you fop! — if you're short, you know why!
  One hundred złoty's nothing for him to waste
Upon a coat, thus on and on you chase...
  And then there's he, who'll squeeze his ample girth
Into an ulan's costume — what that's worth,
  Just take a gander at the collar — fur,
Inside and out. Address him, now, as 'sir,'
  For if you don't, you cad, you'll get what for!
He squanders piles, but think you he keeps score?
  He'll fling in largesse his very last mite
To peasant, cringing churl, and parasite;
  He needs no porter, for his every door
Is closely watched by sharp-eyed creditor,
  And it's the favour of such a one you crave?
For him you labour! You become his slave!
  Greater the titles now, fatter the purse.
As for nobility? So much the worse.
  These days who builds a Palace? What lord founds
A cloister, or the quit-rent from his grounds
  Gives to the king, as did your great forebears,
To whom the nation's good meant more than theirs.
  Today, you take more than you give the King;
With father rector, it's much the same thing.
  'He's wine enough for Mass!' to hear you talk,
You'd think a benefice fleeces the flock!
  'You papist!' 'How d'you know?' 'From what you've said!'
(I'd swear it was the horns upon my head).
  But on Faith's articles I'll not dispute:
I readily confess I'm much too rude.
  Yet I know one thing: a good Christian's not
An orator or learned polyglot,
  But one who keeps God's precepts all his days.

Such a good Christian I will ever praise.
  If your view of these things is different,
Show what you're made of! Off with you to Trent!
  Tell me, how did the old Poles grip the sword
Upon hearing the Gospel of the Lord?
  You think they wasted much time in debate?
(But that's a horny syllogism, hard to explicate).
  Here's what they thought: 'These truths are beyond me.
It's not for me to plumb God's mysteries.
  But once made whole by Baptism's sacred laver
My duty is to serve my loving Saviour.
  I know His Word, to Him I owe my all;
In Him I'll stand fast, till in death I fall.'
  Tell him his faith is faulty! Soon you'll see
Why I would rather stand with such as he!
  I studied neither in Leipzig nor Prague,
Nor listened to Genevan demagogue
  Explain the faith; all that I've understood
I gleaned from hermits living in deep wood
  And barren mountain summit, who impart
The sort of faith that takes root in the heart.
  And it took root in mine as well, despite
The fact I had to overcome my fright,
  For I was taken for a god, you see,
And Bacchus, he was always good to me.
  Nothing, without my counsel, he'd decide;
Why, at his wedding I sat at his side,
  As close as Ariadne — yes, it's true;
And what went through my head then, if you knew,
  Bacchus, my friend! But in time each petty god
Went off to the long sleep beneath the sod,
  And our kind were dispersed about the woods,
Both far and wide, to fend as best we could.
  At last, I was baptised, and made my way
To where more holy customs reign (let's say).
  Back in those days there was no greed at all
Such as today, with worries great and small
  To eat one's heart out; back then no one came

A-cropper chasing wealth; all vied for fame,
　Which neither rare wines nor fat dinners breeds
But only is obtained by noble deeds.
　And as one's worth was not measured in sums,
No shyster won renown by flapping gums!
　For virtue, and not statute, then held sway,
Ensuring concord; justice was fair play.
　But now that men of wealth have had a taste,
Virtue and honour have been banished, chased
　Off to shiver, outcasts, ceding place
To shameless libel and conniving slurs,
　For which, of course, you'll need your barristers.
Such was their ancient use to share no table
　With scoundrels; should one sit down, men were able
To slice the cloth before him, as a sign
　That here was one suspected of a crime.
They'd rap their plates, and should he remain there,
　They'd rise and hurl him out upon his ear!
Today no murderer, traitor, or thief
　Lacks a glib lawyer who will take his brief;
Your women are much nobler creatures, for
　No honest maid will sit beside a whore.
Her mother teaches this, from her first days,
　Which, God's my witness, deserves deathless praise.
But you — what have you from your fathers? Dander
　— Sometimes — should your name be tainted by slander;
For truth they held in highest veneration
　And passed that worship to this generation.
Hold fast to her, accept all that she's given,
　For her abode is nowhere else but Heaven.
Now, is it proper, having left behind
　Old ways, as novel more to taste you find,
That still you hold to ancient compacts so,
　To which you'd have the king himself bow low?
Such things suit nations that preserve the peace
　And concord between peers, whose squabblings cease
When set before a neighbour or a friend
　To judge the suit and bring it to an end,

JAN KOCHANOWSKI

Without involving His Majesty's court
　In trifles; but with fellows of this sort,
Sedulous scoundrels, who so multiply
　Their slurs and suits, and to Parliament fly
Like little children wronged, and their example
　— O petty landowner! — you follow; so ample
The docket groans at sittings, before long
　What man is able to split right from wrong?
The choice is yours: you can't have it both ways:
　Go with the times, or, as in olden days.
It's not for satyrs to debate your laws,
　But let him speak, whoever's got the jaws.
I speak according to my inborn wit.
　Who would say otherwise, speak. Let's hear it.
But let me finish, let me have my say,
　And pardon me if I should over-stray.
And yet I've heard the same things said of you:
　You lose your way before you're half-way through
An argument; why, in the Sejm they say
　It takes a month, what used to take a day;
'Twas thus a foreign fist your Połock grabbed:
　You Poles, instead of fighting, jawed and gabbed.
But I'm no better, for the faults I blame
　In others, well, I have them just the same.
Why is it that you send to Italy
　Your sons for schooling? Or to Germany,
While you've your own universities here
　To which those nations rushed, in bygone years?
You think your Masters simple fieldhands?
　Just wait — soon they'll all be Gregorians
If you refuse them even such a jot
　As now you pay them for their toil of thought;
Pay them what they deserve — you'll see your sons
　Taught better than in all the world's Sorbonnes.
Invest in your children! And when you're through
　All Padua will come clamouring to you.
Is it for manners that one sends a lad
　Abroad? There's manners good, and manners bad

He'll find there. As to which ones he'll prefer
   To your own better lights I here defer.
I'm dense, and yet one thing I understand:
   Nothing's brought so much change into this land
As what you teach your children by example.
   It's far from my desire roughshod to trample
Your way of doing things, which every nation
   Does well to pass down through each generation,
Upon which bases, with time, they shall build
   A world more stable than had they been thrilled
And led by novelty. 'You didn't learn
   That in the woods!' You'll say, but I in turn:
'No, you're mistaken.' For indeed I did!
   All this I have from Chiron, strange hybrid
Of man and horse, tutor of Achilles,
   Whose school was a cave sunk amidst the trees —
Rustic academy, for sure! And yet
   He lagged behind no professor in wit;
And if you like, I'll rattle this old head
   And recollect what the wise centaur said.
'My son,' for so he called his pupil, 'here
   In this retreat, you never need to fear
Any harsh words, or any vulgar sight.
   But there will come a day when you'll take flight
Like a young eaglet, who abandons home,
   His father's care and labours, far to roam,
To find himself among such men as speak
   In vulgar jargon — O, beware their cheek
And bawdy customs, which are nothing worth,
   Lest filth befoul your wings, and bind you fast to earth.
Let vulgar joys your high mind not induce
   To part from honest pleasures, and, seduced
By traitorous sweets to gain a lowly taste
   For meats that nourish not, corrupt and base.
Keep ever in your mind these words: Take care
   To call to mind that God is everywhere,
And sees all things that any man will do —
   Each taint of sin, each glimmer of virtue.

                                        JAN KOCHANOWSKI

And so, before you scheme up anything,
    Remember: God's your witness, and so bring
Your mind the Lord's intentions to fulfil
    In harmony — yours, with His holy, will.
'Twas not by hazard that each beast was formed
    Bent to the earth, while man alone was born
To walk upright, his face toward the skies,
    To scan the measured heavens with bright eyes:
This too a sign bestowed by God on man,
    Revealing to us His eternal plan —
With man and beast fashioned in varied measure,
    As beasts seek only comfort, fleshly pleasure;
To man, whose soul was formed in highest Heaven
    The contemplation of the skies was given.
Be this your only care, your daily plan —
    How to return to that high fatherland
Where dwell immortals. Son, be not like them
    Who their vocations, God's great gift, contemn,
To wallow in the sty like common beasts
    Filling their stomachs full with filthy feasts.
No, virtue imitate, though it demands
    Time, effort, and eludes impatient hands.
Whatever you lose in virtue's pursuit
    Will be repaid, with fame and Heaven to boot.
A free man born, to such whom fortune gave
    Direction over servant, serf, or slave,
Before beginning to rule others, learn
    To rule yourself, and greed and anger spurn.
For you will find your servants more inclined
    To serve a master who's mastered his own mind.
Know that in man's soul some dark powers sit —
    Not only varied, indeed: opposite —
Like ready haste, desire unsatisfied,
    Faint piety, bitter tears, and gladness snide,
Which reason, like some hetman strict and frank
    Commands, lest any fall out of its rank.
Trust in that leader, all your thought confide
    In him, that you be safely fortified.

If to that colonel you your life entrust
  You'll never stray from the path straight and just;
For neither battlements nor stout armed men
  Your health and honour can better defend
Than can your folk's devotion, and their good faith,
  To which Hell's hurricanoes are a breath
Harmless; with goodness and with empathy
  Advancement comes; progress with amity.
Love well your friends, and gratefully pay heed
  To their advice. 'Tis priceless gear indeed:
Monarchs are masters of much wealth, for sure —
  But in the truth they frequently are poor.
So let your ear incline not readily
  To the deceptive sweets of flattery,
Which like a deformed looking glass reflects
  As pretty things the ugliest defects.
The upright man seeks not to whitewash vice.
  Love virtue: from such soil great kingdoms rise,
Where good are honoured, evil quake with fear,
  And what is needed most: examples clear
Abound, for subjects take — in everything —
  Their cues from the behaviour of their king
And master. And you likewise, take good care
  Well to assess your servants' talents; fair
Be always in apportioning their tasks.
  Work must be shared by many; Nature asks
No man to do all toil. No pedigree
  Is worth a jot when one would sail the sea.
If one knows not how to read wind and star,
  Though bluest be his blood, he won't get far.
Above all, never place the greedy there,
  Where office can be bartered! For where
Justice is up for sale, men live accursed:
  The Lord God heeds the wails of the wronged, first.
Should it be given you to compose pacts
  Of peace, beware always the sly attack.
For if I can read the heavens aright,
  The prudent Greek is always primed to fight.

       JAN KOCHANOWSKI

Behold the bandit, who'd make wife to whore!
  See him drag oaken trunks down to the shore
To build new galleys, and repair the old:
  He pins the oars, and soon hoists sail, bold
In his plans to loot that, what would most please
  His lust — O, that he'd never come to Greece!
Or, coming, found another concubine!
  For his pleasure won't last. Soon comes the time
For the winged Spartan to make for the shore
  He fled back to, with death for ware, and war!
No help to him then, sweetly humming strings,
  Smooth cheeks, or locks teased thickly into rings!
He'll dump her from his lap, and in wild fear
  Race, as from the fierce wolf the skittish deer.
In such a case, then you must take a stand
  And under God, defend your slighted land.
Become used now to toil and adverse climes,
  That you'll be strong when faced with trying times.
Learn how the sword to wield, the bow to bend,
  How to pierce others, and yourself defend,
How to surmount trench, ford a river's course,
  How to mount quickly and to rule a horse;
Learn how to bear the swelter and the sleet;
  Spurn wine for water, have bread for your meat;
Though young, strive now betimes to understand
  How you will lead the men you shall command,
How to choose the best place to bivouac,
  And how — wisely — your foe to best attack.
Learn how in ranks your men must be arrayed
  That they might come to one another's aid,
And if your enemy be fortified,
  Learn how to raise a rampart on your side
Stout, strong, equal to his in height
  To lend him no advantage in the fight;
Learn how to fill the fosse that steeply falls
  And how to fashion rams to smash his walls;
How them to undermine with pioneers —
  A great work, which one doesn't learn by ears,

But brawn and daring. Son, though you be young,
  Train now with blade, yes, have your longbow strung
And train to equal what you've learned from story —
  Surpassing even your forefathers' glory.
No mortal can escape his destined end.
  Strive now for glory, rather than to spend
Your youth in luxury and idleness,
  Never to learn what life offers the best.
The future's in God's hands. But you — despite
  Your ignorance of fate — do what is right.
Virtue breeds fame, and in ages to come,
  God shall inspire one to keep always young
And green your glorious fame; his pen of gold
  Will teach all nations that the ages hold
No valour topping yours. Undying fame
  Will bruit forever more Achilles' name.'
With such sweetmeats the aged centaur fed
  His charge, while nearby I inclined my head
Listening, though never did I dare suspect
  His words prophetic would have such effect
On history… But where's my wit! For you
  Shoo me with brooms while I preach on virtue.
Far better had I lectured you instead
  On what your future holds, to fill you with dread…
But what will come, will come, as you shall see
  Once from your forecourts you've made me to flee —
With sure, though leaden tread comes plodding Care:
  Wise they, who use the time lent to prepare.

TO THE SATYR

Dear Satyr, as you wander through our clime
  Back to your woods, stop by from time to time
And tell me how the world is treating you —
  (Not everyone would thrash you black and blue;
There are such as will heed you, and give thanks —
  Each nation has wise men as well as cranks);
I'd gladly learn my faults, a harsher doom
    To slip — and look! I greet you with no broom…

DRAMATIC WORKS

The Dismissal of the Grecian Envoys

Alcestis Took her Husband's Place in Death

Guesses

THE DISMISSAL OF THE GRECIAN ENVOYS

(1577)

To my most Gracious Lord, Jan Zamoyski of Zamość, Under-chancellor Royal, etc., etc., with an offering of my humble services.

Just yesterday I received both letters, which my Lord wrote me concerning this play of mine. I was pleasantly surprised to receive them, for after such a long time I had reckoned that the tragedy was to be consigned to the ages as well, or, more precisely, was to become food for moths or funnels for apothecaries. When I read my Lord's letters, there was no time for tidying up the draught, for I had to *insumere* my all on copying it out. *Quicquid id est*, and I fear that it is but silliness, and that my Lord will be of the same opinion, I still send it to him, and all the more boldly now, although I needs must warn him beforehand that it was not written *ad amussim*, as such was beyond the scope of the author's talents. What's more, it doesn't strike the ear well. *Inter caetera,* there are three choruses, and the third would imitate the Greek chorus, a separate *characterem* as is the case with them… I don't know how it will sound in our language. But in this (really, in everything) I beg that the *arbitrium* be my Lord's. I would like nothing better than, *praesens* my Lord, to offer him my service, but ill health will not permit me to do so. Alas, if but *salus* would allow! Casting myself upon my Lord's mercy, I am

My Gracious Lord's
      most willing servant,
           Jan Kochanowski

Dat. in Czarnolas the twenty-second of December in the year of Our Lord MDLXXVII.

THE PERSONS

Antenor
Alexander, *also known as Paris*
Helen
Old Woman
Ulysses, *Grecian envoy*
Menelaus, *Grecian envoy*
Priam, *King of Troy*
Cassandra
Coast Guard
Prisoner
Chorus *of Trojan maidens.*

The scene is set in Troy.

PROLOGUE

ANTENOR
That which I've often felt and said aloud,
That insult and wrongdoing of such measure
Could not be suffered by the warlike Greeks
Has come to pass: Their envoys now are here,
Who will exact of us Helen's return.
She who was stolen away over quick-backed seas
By Paris, Priam's son — unfaithful guest:
Filched from her lord and brazened here to Troy.
If we return her to her husband's hands
We shall sit fast in an unbroken peace.
But if the envoys return as they have come,
The horizon blackens with a Grecian fleet.
The scent of tar has reached sweet Paris' nose:
Calls in old debts, and goes 'round slapping backs;
Sends little gifts… nor have I been forgotten.
But I and my house, this my father's house
Are not for sale. Defend me, God, from this —
That I should sling my name from market hooks!

The man who would have gold speak in his stead
Does not believe in his own righteousness.
Yet also he is void of reasoning
Who will take bribes, as if but he himself
Were to be whole, while all else perishes.
But now it's time to work. Today the king
Is to receive the envoys. But… Paris, here?

EPEISODION I

(Alexander, Antenor)

ALEXANDER

Antenor! Friend! True as a friend is true!
Come now, promise, as the others have
That you, just Antenor, will stand by me,
And uphold my cause against the Greek.

ANTENOR

Willingly shall I, honoured Prince, uphold
The cause of righteousness, and benefit
To our Republic.

ALEXANDER

        No excuses now!
Not when a friend comes calling with a suit!

ANTENOR

Of course, indeed — if but the suit be just.

ALEXANDER

To wish the stranger well, and curse one's friend,
Stinks just a mite of jealousy.

ANTENOR

           But to serve
A friend while scorning honour and holy truth —
This stinks just a mite of knavery.

ALEXANDER

One hand
Washes the other, one leg
Supports his fellow, as the friend's a port to friend.

ANTENOR
A great friend is to be found in honesty:
Nor are demands the use of friendly speech.

ALEXANDER
In need, they say, one comes to know one's friend.

ANTENOR
Conscience, they say, points out the friend in need.

ALEXANDER
What lovely conscience — to stand by a friend!

ANTENOR
Lovelier yet is that which stands by truth.

ALEXANDER
Your truth is to give succour to the Greeks!

ANTENOR
All men are Greek who live by righteousness.

ALEXANDER
You're very quick to pass sentence on me.

ANTENOR
The constant is a harsh, impartial judge.

ALEXANDER
Impartial? Why your house is full of Greeks!

ANTENOR

My door will never close before a Greek
Or Trojan, if he be an honest man.

ALEXANDER

Yes, yes — and if he's got a whorish purse.

ANTENOR

Go easy, Paris. I must needs bribe a judge.
I stole a wife, and her lord's lawyer's glib.

ALEXANDER

I know nothing of your wife, but gifts you have —
Gifts from the Greeks! Mine own will not suffice.

ANTENOR

I spoke in jest.
Both gifts and strange wives I am loth to take.
Yet as you live, I see, so do you speak:
Be gone — I want nothing to do with you.

ALEXANDER

I'm sorry I came here. I'll trust the gods
And, in despite of your miserly grace,
I'll find someone to link his shield with mine.

ANTENOR

One such as yourself.

ALEXANDER

God will it — an honest man!

CHORAL ODE I

CHORUS

For wisdom to be set in youth,
Nor hath the sea a horde of pearls in sooth,

Nor is there gold enough in mountain pit
To barter for the young an ounce of wit.

Less sorrows would there be to rue
If one could but unite the two.
Their lusts would run to better ends,
No springe would trip them up, nor trap their friends!

As it is, they think with gut and prick
While their mind's grown dull and sick;
They melt their gold on mercury,
And the Republic pays the highest fee.

Eternal God, who rulest earth and sky,
The price Thou'st set for wisdom sure is high:
Wit for youth; perhaps a happy trade,
But what fond sorrow when the deal is made!

Look — Helen comes. What now runs through her mind
To think that the Assembly sits today
To seal her fate — is she to stay in Troy?
Or will she grace the Spartan shore again?

EPEISODION II

(Old Woman, Helen)

HELEN
I saw it all as in a looking glass:
Not long was he to revel in his prize,
The scoundrel Paris, whom the noble Greeks
Should have set to his lessons long ago!
Yet he, like a starved wolf breaking the fold,
Escaped in haste while they, like shepherds, chased
After the thief with dogs. Soon must the wolf
Let drop the ewe from his foam-flecked jaws
And, humbled, race into the woods alone.
Now what, unfortunate, will be my lot?

An iron halter fixed to the rough deck
Of the most central Grecian ship of war.
What face will greet my longing brother's eyes?
How may I, shameless, stand before your visage,
My sweetest husband? Shall I skip to you,
And laugh? And boldly stroke your iron cheek?
Would that you'd never seen the Spartan shore,
Unhappy Priamid! What did I lack?
Daughter of princes, married to a king,
God-given beauty, children, and a good name —
That above all! Now all of this is lost
Thanks to that evil man! So far from home,
No friends, not knowing if my children live,
Myself no better than a slave, subject
To glancing rumour, ill repute — What still
Fortune will start with me, God only knows!

OLD WOMAN
Now, now — don't beat your breast like that, my dear.
Such is the nature of our life: now joy,
Now sadness. From these two our lives are spun.
Delights spring on us unawares, but woes
Must come, when God wills, or the times dictate.

HELEN
O mother dear, unequal is the weft
Of this dark garland; far more wormwood's in it
Than roses — far more hemlock than daisies.

OLD WOMAN
It only seems so, Lady Helena:
One readily takes bad tidings to heart
And is more sceptical when good news comes.
Thus it will seem as if there's more of that
Which saddens, than that which gladdens, man's life.

HELEN

No, no — The bad outweighs the good. Consider but
The one unvaried birth which brings all men
Into the world, against the manifold
And divers ways he has of leaving it.
Thus is his health unique — but mortal man
Is plagued by numberless strains of disease.
And even she, who rules the fate of all,
Fortune, will take my part! Consider too
How sparse the gold — which men do covet most —
And slippery! No sooner in the grasp,
But sliding out to rattle on the ground,
Whence it attracts some future beggar's eye.
Leave off your well-intended poetry.

OLD WOMAN

Less good, more ill, or equal both — who knows?
And small indeed the profit to discover.
Pray God, rather, that Fortune's changing winds
Buffet you from both sides. Anything else
Is inhuman. But come now — go inside.
I'm sure that Paris will, without delay,
Send some news of the late deliberations.
So come, the hearth is a more fitting place
For women like us, than the public square.

CHORAL ODE II

CHORUS

May they who the Res Publica defend
And fondle human justice in their hand,
Set up as shepherds of god-fashioned folk
To lead to freedom, not drive beneath the yoke,

Recall, that they repose on purple thrones
Through God's will — through no merit of their own.

JAN KOCHANOWSKI

May they be mindful of their holy charge
To serve not themselves, but the state at large.

When the assembly opens with the marshal's bell,
May't call them to govern their own selves, as well.
May they remember that a higher Court
Judges the acts of men of every sort.

Let no man take a bribe, nor seek to trace
The lineage of him who pleads his case;
Whether he bears a mattock or a sword,
If he's a fault, let chains be his reward.

Let them take care, for when the vulgar sins,
The cancer of his crime ends where it begins.
But when a leader's crimes burst into bloom,
Whole cities and whole empires fall to ruin.

EPEISODION III
(Messenger, Helen)

MESSENGER
I come with good tidings for my lady.
I know that she's long waited on this news,
Bruising her heart with cares and heavy tears.
That's her before her house now! O, my queen!
The bearer of good tidings kneels before you.

HELEN
God grant indeed that your tidings be good.

MESSENGER
The Greek envoys depart as they had come:
They leave our shores, and you remain with us.

HELEN
Your information — is it second hand?

MESSENGER

I was myself within the Senate house,
Then Alexander bade me come to you.

HELEN

I still don't know of what I should be glad.
What happened, then?

MESSENGER

                      Listen! I'll tell you all.
As soon as all the lords were seated,
The king addressed them with these very words:
'Assembled lords, it has not been my use
To plot a course without consulting you,
Sure stars of our Republic's firmament;
And even if (and I recall it not)
I've ever moved to do so, in this case,
Which touches my own son (and blood, they say,
Is thicker far than water), I will not
That one man's will should drive him on the rocks,
With so many good pilots near at hand.
The more so, since the matter stretches past
One man's fate or desires, and weighs upon
The whole of our Republic. Grave indeed
And portentous the present moment. Troy,
Whatever twist you give the rudder, I
Will trust the ship of state into your hands.
My son, it seems, got him a wife in Greece.
How he came by her, this I do not know.
But these Greek envoys demand her return.
So, give her back? Or no? Well then, my lords!
Such is the task before you.' He had done,
Then Paris rose, and thus began to speak:
'My father, at the envoys' first complaint,
I gave a full accounting of myself,
My actions. Now I would not tire your ears
With empty words, but first shall throw myself
On God's will, and on your mercy, and the wit

                                                         JAN KOCHANOWSKI

Of these judicious men. It's known to all
That I have led a clean and blameless life.
I could never bear to look on drunken brawls,
But hastened to the deepest oaken glades
To hunt the antlered stag and wild boar.
Nor did I account it hardship to repose
In a shepherd's hovel; nor did I dream
Of Helen then — nor had I heard the name!
Venus — when chosen by the goddesses
Judge of their beauty — Venus herself
First recommended and gave me my wife.
I see how people beg a boon of God —
When, pleading not, one was bestowed on me,
What then? Should I spurn it in contempt?
I took her! And I took with gratitude!
It is my dearest wish, that that same goddess
Who blest me then, will bless me all my days,
And shield her gift from jealous, grasping hands.
And even had I won my wife as men
Are used to do — I cannot see wherefore
The villain who raped Medea from her home
Should escape your censure, while I am called to task
For a like misdemeanour. Am I guilty?
Then so is he. The Greeks want gifts?
Let them be givers first, as penalty
For the more ancient crime. Now, in that case,
Give back my wife, and hand me over too!
Dear father! I'll gladly bear the penance!
For if they feel that everyone owes them
Just measure, themselves owing nothing, by God,
They'll have no easy traffic here, by words
Or by the sword! I can't believe
That you've forgotten, father, the old wrongs
Suffered of these lords and their famous land.
Still lie the broken scarps along the sand,
And cornfields to this day as desert wastes
Bear witness to Greek cruelty and deceit.
Hesione must remember — your sister,

My aunt — who to this very day
Languishes in their slavery... if she's still alive.
That sole harm no one Helen will repay,
Nor single Paris effect just revenge.'
Young Alexander finished, and a buzz
Whispered about the hall, as in late Summer,
When worker bees will murmur in the hive,
Choosing a chief to lead them from the queen
And towards a new home. Just such muttering
Arose among the lords. When it died down,
Antenor stood up, and began to speak:
'Your Majesty, what need we beat our pates
With lengthy proofs? The matter stands thus:
Paris, in Greece, being the guest of one
Of kingly estate, the laws of hospitality
Uncomprehending, stole from him a wife.
Does a good, honest man, do such shameful things?
He is not free of debt. Menelaus —
Ashamed himself — perhaps for Paris, too —
Asks her return, and this I do advise,
So that we bear no part in your son's crime.
And mark you all — the Greeks will have her back —
If not with words, then with that sword
Which silly Paris underestimates.
Let Paris woo a less expensive bride,
Who brings not war and death as dowry.
If he trusts so fully in that goddess' grace,
Let him now fear those other two, whose ire
Was stirred by his most venal judgemanship.
Medea was not stolen in our time,
Nor do I know if this is cause for strife.
Have any of you sent envoys to the Greeks
Requiring her return? Your fathers, too,
Kept silent, and 'twas they were robbed, not you.
These are schoolchildren's pranks, who mewl and bawl,
Pointing their finger at another's chest.
It's true — the Greeks once laid our city low.
But even then, lord, and truth must be told,

'Twas our unrighteousness that sped our ruin.
Thus am I frightened, King and men of Troy,
Lest there be some god's harsh decree in this,
That our injustice should find its working out
Beneath the stern rod of the patient Greeks.
Nor is it out of place that I remind
Your Majesty that, in that first defeat,
You nearly lost your life in penance for
Your father's guilt and less than righteous deeds.'
Then he grew quiet. Aeneas agreed,
As did Tymethes, and Panthus, and Lampon,
And Ukalegon too. But Iktaon
Saw it another way, and thus he spoke:
'Antenor, tell me: would you have us skip
To every tune plucked on the Grecian lute?
You bid us fear them, and indeed I do!
Today it's Helen they demand, tomorrow
It will be our own wives and our own children.
Greed does not hold itself in check, but is
Like to a river at the flooding stage:
Creeps up the earthwork unnoticeably,
To spill unbridled down the dike in rage,
Consuming all, carrying all away.
Now is the time, my lords, to shut the locks,
For when the deluge comes, it stifles all.
As for the good faith of these "patient Greeks" —
They beg for justice, blackmailing us with war.
"Give us Helen, or we'll tear her from your hands..."
We should have justice, but justice without shame!
Who seeks it thus would have not recompense
Alone, but our opprobrium as well.
Justice, and righteousness — mere weightless words
Until iron's hung on 'em. The Greeks
Would style themselves alone civilised lords,
And like to call us Trojans *barbaroi*.
Mere birth in Ithaca makes no man a lord
Nor does the soil of Troy engender slaves.
Noble is he who wields the sharper blade.

And if the matter comes to bronze on hide,
Then we'll just see who bows down before whom.
Till then we shall be equals. Let the Greeks
Save all their ranting and look to themselves.
If there's wrong in this, Paris raping Helen,
Then they're complicit in the crime as well,
For they first showed him how to get a girl.
Nor did Paris steal brother and sister
As did the Greeks, when they bore off with force
Medea and Absyrtos with her.
And Antenor would say that that's all right,
That we could not care less. Bah! not care more!
They wish to finger us with such filthy hands?
I don't think so. And what's good for Europe
Holds true for Asia too. Now and forever.
As for the sister of the king, old wrongs
Are not forgotten, where Trojan blood's concerned.
Thus, in the name of vengeance, let's keep Helen
Until the Greeks return Medea to us.'
Those were his words. Then, no one wished to waste
Their breath with further speech. They spoke as one:
'Yes, Iktaon's right.' Though several times
Ukalegon rose, their roar drowned him out.
The marshals beat their staffs upon the ground:
'Listen my lords — Ukalegon would speak!'
But not even those thumps could help him, and
Ukalegon spoke to Ukalegon.
Then someone shouted this proposal out:
'What good are petty speeches? Let's vote now
And see where we all stand.' He hardly spoke
When all sprang to their feet and chose their place.
When they divided, counting was redundant:
Most stood by Paris, and but a handful
Took Menelaus' side. They bade the king
Decree what the majority determined,
And he, without delay, then spoke these words:
'I would have been glad, had unanimity
Been the outcome of these consultations,

But, despite the lack of concord, I must,
As sovereign ruler of the realm of Troy
Abide your will and accordingly find
In Paris' favour, charging thus the Greeks
To forfeit Helen in Medea's place.'
Right after this, the envoys were dismissed
And Alexander sent me here to tell you
All that I heard. The envoys go back home,
And, as before your husband waits in Sparta
Upon your return. And let him wait, I say!

HELEN
And you say well. Go forth, I'll follow you.

EPEISODION IV
(Chorus, Ulysses, Menelaus)

CHORUS
It seems his story suits her well. But not me —
Nor am I sure that this will bring her joy.
Look: the envoys come with gloomy faces:
It's plain to see things didn't go as planned.

ULYSSES
O lawless kingdom, near calamity!
Where neither truth is loved, nor righteousness
Has place, but all stinks of the market square!
Where wastrels such as this, with metal chips
Can win the most exalted of the land
To paint his lechery a virtue, gild
His scoundrel's burglary a patriotic quest!
Since you will not see the truth, beware the end
To which this all must lead in consequence.
Can you not understand, nor intimate
How cancerous this lechery is to the state?
Virtue and shame bear merchant's tags
And Good swims into Evil's foul embrace —

Like fatal stars in the heavens boding ruin.
Thus houses crumble, thus the state is sucked
Of blood and totters — Troy! You will prove it out! —
Thus men are stripped of their humanity
Becoming beasts after the fashion of beasts
Whose glutted bellies drag along the floor.
Look: see the trains of parasites, with whom
The streets are strewn in a parade of greed
Marking the paths the dogs trot down, like scraps
Of offal fallen from their laden maws.
From this lot, think you that even one will prove
An asset to his fatherland in war?
How will he bear his armour, whom the load
Of silk and satin throws into a swoon?
How will he stand on watch, who's used to drowse
The heavy afternoons away? How breast
With foes, whose drunken feet trace arabesques?
With such as these on guard — and not on guard —
They call for war! May it so please Thee, God,
That I shall always spar with such as these!

MENELAUS
Eternal lights of heaven, fecund earth,
And you, broad sea, and you gods, high and low,
Bear witness to me now! I came to Troy
With a just suit, to right my grievous wrongs
And great disgrace, yet leave unsatisfied,
With no reward save jeers and a heavier heart.
Thus do I lay my insults and my wrongs
At your feet, mighty gods. If with pure heart
I pray to you, you will avenge my shame
And wrongs too plain! Give me the throat
Of Alexander to straddle, the thin blood
Of that dishonourable wretch to slake
The thirst of my sword. For far too long has he
Been glutted with my shame, as he feeds on it now!

CHORAL ODE III

CHORUS

O white-winged swimmer of the wine-dark sea,
Foster-daughter of tall-masted Ida,
Beech bark, which through the salty seaways
Carried the smooth cheeks of the Priamid
To the transparent fords of Achaia!
What hast thou brought the daughters of Priam,
Esteemed Polyxenes and Cassandra,
What, for a sister-in-law?
A bride whose footsteps piqued the speeding hounds
Foaming after her, a slave escaping!
Can this be she, the promised boon of Venus,
Given in token for the crooked verdict
Tossed down by Paris at the foot of Ida?
Strife and contention were your matchmakers,
You false boy, you corruptive referee!
I would not harbour ill bodings in my breast,
But cannot keep my bloody thoughts in check:
This will come to no good.
O, Queen of Cyprus, may I never desire
Another man than him who shares my bed!
Greedy eyes lead to ruptured guts.
But he who holds desire by the bit
Will spend his days in bliss and opulence.
They come, they come, the days of smoke and fire;
War will in, and steal from the slumberer
His sweetest fantasies, and shake the beating heart
With trumpets wailing beneath the battlements,
And Grecian darts eroding Pergamum.

EPEISODION V
(Antenor, Priam, Cassandra, Chorus)

ANTENOR

Since solid counsel could not move Your Majesty

To send Helena back where she belongs
And thus extinguish quickly the hot brand
Of this great war which — doubt it not! — now looms
Above our heads, I urge Your Majesty:
Prepare your kingdom for the certain onslaught,
As sure to come as now I stand before you.
You heard yourself the envoys' dark farewell:
Now from our own tributaries come reports
Of Grecian hoplites making haste to Aulis.
No doubt their destination is your unhappy realm.
Why else would they have sent their deputies
Who spoke so rawly of their injury?
Thus, as we still securely hold our shoreline,
Send men and brass to the outlying ports
And fortresses. Order dependent princes
To stand at ready; call your soldiers up;
Send out your spies and guard the land and sea
So that the eager Greeks may not find you
For combat unprepared. This is my counsel.

PRIAM
And are you so afraid, good Antenor?
As if you saw the enemy without!

ANTENOR
My lord, now is the proper time to fear!
From such anxiety springs readiness.
Deliberations now are useless. Fight,
Or run away. You have no third recourse.

PRIAM
Well, yes, I wish to have all taken care of
So that there be no need for sudden flight.

ANTENOR
Which God forbid! But look — who is this woman
With hair dishevelled, with a face so pale?
Her limbs are twitching, and her breath comes hard,

JAN KOCHANOWSKI

She heaves her breast; her eyes roll in her head,
She makes to speak, then stops her mouth…

PRIAM

My daughter,

Unfortunate Cassandra. Mad again.
Possessed by Apollo. Nothing we can do.
We have to hold our peace and let her rave.

CASSANDRA

Why do you vainly torment me, Apollo,
Who, having given me this prophetic sight,
Refuse my words due weight? My oracles
Are as the wind, and people give them heed
No more than empty tales and fleeting dreams.
Who will be aided by my heart possessed,
Or my afflicted mind? My borrowed soul
And senses, ruled by you, overbearing guest?
I cannot throw you off; I'm being raped!
I cannot rule myself; I'm not my own.
But where am I, by God? I see no light;
A sudden night has blotted out my eyes.
I see… two suns; I see… two Pergamums;
I see… a doe swimming in the deep sea.
Unhappy doe! That doe's an evil omen!
You! Shepherds! Go guard the shallows! Prevent
The fatal guest from swimming to the shore!
Unhappy the land, unhappy the strand
Where that doe sets her foot! Unhappy wood
Where she lays down her smooth flanks in repose.
Each of her hoofprints, every nest of hers
Will brim with blood! She carries in her train
Destruction, firestorm, and desolation.
O my fair homeland! O, god-fashioned walls!
What end awaits you? O, my brother, guardian
Of Troy and pillar of this noble house!
Thessalian horses champ to drag you round
The ramparts of your city, while your sire,

The king, become a beggar, kneels to buy
Your corpse from the cruel bandit who killed you!
But you too, heartless butcher, you will fall,
Shot through by a dart from an unmanly bow.
What then? The tree is felled, but from the trunk
A new sprig shall push forth, and beyond hope
The heavens will ascend! But ah, that horse —
So huge! And standing in the field alone?
Don't lead him to the stables! Keep him hence,
If you don't wish to burn them to the ground!
That night will be as is the brightest day,
And nothing will be seen then, come the dawn.
O, father, then trust not your household gods,
Nor wrap your arms around the holy altars —
A cruel lion's cub snaps at your heels!
He will imprison you in his sharp claws
And slake his parched throat with your aged heart's blood!
Your sons all slaughtered, all your daughters slaves,
There will be no one left to bury the dead!
Mother, you will not weep over your children,
But you will howl!

CHORUS

                              Come with me! Let us take
The crazy woman to some other room...

EPILOGUE
(*Antenor, Priam*)

ANTENOR
Not hard to understand those words, my king:
Clearly, the nation's ruin they foretell,

And yours as well. For God's sake, Majesty,
Don't treat them lightly, like an old wives' tale!

PRIAM

She has not quite implanted fear in me
With this her fatal croaking. Though, I admit
She scared me somewhat… for they call to mind
A curious dream that plagued Queen Hecuba
My wife, some years ago, when she was heavy
With Alexander in her youthful womb.
She dreamt that she'd brought forth no laughing child,
But a flaming firebrand.

ANTENOR

                  Yes, I remember,
And I recall the priests' interpretation:
That child was to work out Troy's destruction,
Something which I see coming, quickly, now!

PRIAM

You speak well. Would I had the whelp exposed!
The wolves should long ago have torn apart
The embryonic sin, and spread its bones
Upon the hills.

ANTENOR

             Far better had it been
Than we should die today because of him.
But what is this? A captive marched this way,
And by the cloak he wears, it seems, a Greek!

(*Enter Coast Guard, Prisoner*)

COAST GUARD

Well, this is fine, my lords. You banter here,
And in the field the Greeks have launched a war!
Yesterday afternoon, five Grecian galleys
Drew up along the Trojan strand. It's true
They took no hostages, burned nothing,
But stole whatever grazed in the near fields.
As we were small in number, our protests

Were all for naught — a few of ours were slain,
And we have only this one man to show
For the encounter. Under torture, he
Admitted that one thousand troops were poised
At Aulis waiting for propitious winds
To push them Troy-ward. There they wait,
Until their envoys' breath should fill their sails,
Or furl them with calm. Should Helen not arrive
In their company — as we know she won't,
Since they embarked alone — their legions massed
Will soon push off and head for Troy. That's so?

PRISONER
It is.

COAST GUARD
          And under Agamemnon?

PRISONER
                                        Yes.
The brother of dishonoured Menelaus.

PRIAM
Enough. Take him away and lock him up,
And keep him under guard. So now, Antenor,
We have something more tangible than dreams
And fatal gibbering to see the future plain.
Tomorrow morning we shall call the Senate,
Nor shall it be dissolved, until a fit
Defence is drawn up to breast this invasion.

ANTENOR
As I see it, although my bitter words
Sound like a prophecy, each year we've met
To work out a defence! Right now, it's time
To draw up battle plans, determining how
To strike the first blow, not wait for it to fall!

THE END

ALCESTIS TOOK HER HUSBAND'S PLACE IN DEATH

APOLLO

Admetus' house, where I, although a god,
Was made to taste the fare that blackguards swill,
Because of Jupiter — who killed my son
With a swift-winged lightning bolt, for which
In ire I decimated the cyclopes,
Those smiths gigantic, for which my father
Bound me in servitude to mortal man.
That's how I found myself here, herding kine,
Taking my turn through the long nighttime hours
As doorkeep, until now — For my good lord,
Who serves the gods, as this god once served him,
Who serves him one last time, preserving him
From death. For I've prevailed upon the Parcae
To grant Admetus to slip past the grave...
As long as he shall find a substitute
To take his place. But who'd agree to that?
He made a timid circuit of his friends —
They all refused him, as his father did;
As did the mother who gave birth to him.
No one he found, until he asked his wife.
His wife offers her life for him, and now —
I saw her — fainted in her women's arms
Poor thing, about to bid the light farewell.
Today, in fact, her time — his time — runs out:
Alcestis soon must relinquish her soul.
Now... I'm off. I've no wish to witness that;
I leave forever more this pleasant hearth.
I go... but... Here comes someone unwelcome!
Death nears — the princess of all mortal flesh,
To lead Alcestis under the dark soil.
And right on time; she's never tardy, her!
O, how she watched the shadow on the dial
I bet, chiding the lazy gnomon!

DEATH

Why do you linger, Phoebus, at this porch?
What new intrigues are brewing in your head

JAN KOCHANOWSKI

Against the laws of nature? Do you seek
To tear the morsel due us from our grip?
Are you unsatisfied with having wheedled
Admetus from the grave, tripping the Fates
With crooked words? And why the bow
There at your shoulder? Aim you it at me?
Remember: no one made Alcestis vow
To take her husband's place! That was her choice.

APOLLO
You needn't fear violence at my hands.

DEATH
Tell that to Niobe. Lay down that bow.

APOLLO
I always carry it. It's what I do.

DEATH
Like giving treacherous aid to Admetus.

APOLLO
I suffer at my dear friend's misfortune!

DEATH
And so you'd steal from me again, for him?

APOLLO
I didn't steal him from you by brute force!

DEATH
Then why treads he the earth that should him cover?

APOLLO
Because he gives his wife! That's why you've come.

DEATH
And you'll stand by, while I lead her below?

APOLLO

Go! Do what you've come to do. I'm powerless.

DEATH

All men are born to die. That's an old saw.

APOLLO

All men must die — but only when they're old!

DEATH

I know what you're up to; what you yearn for!

APOLLO

Can you not let her be until she's old?

DEATH

I won't. Such things are for me to decide.

APOLLO

What's it to you? One woman more, or less!

DEATH

When they die young, far greater is my glory!

APOLLO

Oldsters are given sumptuous funerals...

DEATH

Respect to persons, Phoebus? Money? You?

APOLLO

What's that? Remember who you're speaking to!

DEATH

If I could be bribed, no rich man would die.

APOLLO

So you won't do me this one grace, one favour?

DEATH

I can't. You know my ways and customs, now…

APOLLO

Horrid to men and hateful to the gods!

DEATH

You waste your breath. Nothing will come of this.

APOLLO

You shall be foiled, be you ever so ghastly!
A man is on his way here, to this house,
From Eurystheus, sent to fetch some steeds
For frigid Thrace, and while he's hosted here
He'll tear the woman from your chill clutches!
Take this as truth oracular. I'll do
Nothing — nor shall you, except curse me, later!

DEATH

Flap on your lips! Your words are impotent!
That woman soon shall slip beneath the soil —
I'm going now to fashion her coiffeur —
She, whose locks I'll trim with this sickle
Is dedicate to the gods underground.

CHORUS

Why has it gone so silent in the court?
Why has the house of Admetus grown dumb?
There is no friend at hand to let us know…
Are we to raise the lament for the girl?
Have we a queen yet, in living Alcestis?
Of all women, all wives, the most faithful,
As I say boldly — as all testify!

GUESSES

Landowner and Rector

LANDOWNER

Well then, Father Rector, do you really see the future of our Republic in such gloomy colours?

RECTOR

Not me alone, your grace, but all people, small as well as great, are saying that it's all over for us. And even if I can't set my finger on a single specific reason for this state of things, the very fact that this is bruited abroad as common knowledge urges us not to lightly dismiss such guesses. Since ancient times people have turned a sharp eye and attentive ear to what is in common circulation, so that whatever all of the people assert, to a man, it's hard to doubt that there's something in it; and thus came about the saying *Vox populi vox Dei*. And in the end even those philosophers who didn't gladly hang their hats on any little thing, but searched out the truth as if following the string that leads to the gnarl, came to believe that God exists, since there is no nation so raw as not to acknowledge His existence.

LANDOWNER

True enough; people have being going round with heavy hearts, at which I myself am hardly cheered, but setting aside these guesses (as you term them) I'd be obliged to hear something more concrete from you.

RECTOR

To speak of future things, your grace, is but a guessing game, because, after all, God is mighty enough to divert the flow of events; in any case, if such is your will, I'll tell you what I understand of this our Republic. Republics decline and fall just as any other thing, and this either because of internal or external causes. Your external causes are violence or foreign enemies. There seem to be more internal causes, but all of these are like little streams that feed the great river of dissension that, when it roars in flood, can tear a nation apart. So, either by internal disaccord does a Republic shred itself apart by its own strength, as happened in the case of the Romans, or it falls into enemy hands, as happened to the Greeks, not that long ago. As far as foreign enemies are concerned, no one is so dull as not to note what sort of neighbours we sit among, and the danger they present, because those who appear to us unfeignedly as enemies (one must speak truly) we are unable to drive

JAN KOCHANOWSKI

back, and those whom we somehow count as our friends, we don't much respect. Before I say anything about our own unruly, fractious thoughts, let us first consider what that greatest Prophet of all had to say concerning a divided state: *Omne — inquit — regnum in se divisum desolabitur.* These words are no far-fetched prophecy as much as they are a description of the peculiar and immutable causes of the destruction of all states. Because though cities and all Republics first are founded upon concord and thus they increase, then again through discord and quarrelling they must fall, as *contraria contrariis facillime dissolvuntur.* With this in mind, let us consider our own situation — have we not lain the foundations of this our Republic with various common laws, which we disturb with faiths at variance? And to touch upon the laws, it is no secret with what quarrelling and feuding and, in the end, with what threats you carry out their 'execution;' and for all that, I see nothing resulting from that Union so far, save reciprocal animosity and dislike. And on the other hand, so that we not only be torn asunder in secular matters, we must differ in things of the spirit as well, tearing ourselves apart into strange and various faiths, which introduce all the more contention among the people! And let us consider that all the wars that in olden days the Christians waged against the pagans arose from nothing other than differences in faith. And these Christian armies, and those forces of the orders of darkness, never fought so furiously over Jerusalem or Constantinople — with Turks and Saracens! — as the Christians today do over Christ and His faith! This natural quarrel, which arises from a difference in faith with the pagans, we abandon, and we turn upon ourselves in our factiousness. Not only do we not seek out Turks in Thrace, or Asia, to fight against, but we turn upon one another, dear Lord!, to wage bloody battles against ourselves, and all because of varied faiths. He who has torn asunder such holy bonds and praiseworthy unity among people is deserving of the greatest curses, to say nothing more. He is worthy of the severest penalties that a Republic can mete out against those who show discord and betray the Republic, to whom unity and security are dear. Because faith and law (begging the pardon of all modern theologians) are seen to strive toward one and the same end: which is the establishment and security of the Republic, and he who rises up against either of these, harms the Republic as a whole. What I say here, that faith and law tend to the same end, which is the firm establishment of the Republic, is in perfect accord with what you hear me and others pronounce from the pulpit in church: it is for this reason that long, long ago the Lord God revealed His will to men, first through the prophets and then through His Son, so that He might be known and praised. For the praise of God results in this, that when all confess to and heed the Lord God in the same manner, we receive of Him not only ghostly blessings, according to the promises He made unto us, but our Republic, on account of unity, becomes a firm defence in this world for ourselves and our descendants. Nor is it seemly for us to think so miserly of the inexhaustible goodness of the Lord and the graces He pours down upon the human race that, forgetting our own good and advantage, we should have nothing in mind save our own glory, or, on the other hand, striving to assure ourselves our future eternal blessedness, we should give no thought to this present life on earth. But as the Lord is good and always favourably inclined to the human race, He has presented us with one path which, if we but keep to it, we shall live here on earth in greater order and security, and after our death, achieve life eternal. And this path is our faith and His sacred teaching. And as I understand it, Cicero's Scipio says nothing against our faith when he states that nothing on earth is more pleasing to God than well-ordered societies, and that is what Republics are. For as He loves the human species, it is probable that He is pleased with all that is most beautiful among men and most to their advantage. And this is more than merely being pleased with something. For just as when an impoverished householder invites a perceptive, wealthy guest to his home, the latter will arrive with gifts that both cheer his host and give witness to his own generosity and honesty, so the Lord God, comprehending that in this well-ordered community, not only is human security made all the more firm, but His praise is also more solidly established, He supports and ensures human laws and legislated customs with His own revelations and teachings. For we cannot call any Republic firmly-grounded and well-ordered where people carry out their duties out of terror of the punishments threatened by the law — for they might sin in order to avoid such punishment. Rather, only there do we find security and good government where, not out of fear, but because of their virtue, people do what they ought. For such as wish both to avoid punishment and do good will never do wrong — and such is the effect that the faith has upon them. Therefore it can be remarked that a proper Republic rests more certainly upon faith than upon law. Laws have authority only upon the flesh, which is by nature subject to other lords, that is, to the senses. But faith moulds the mind. Consequently, faith governs both the human mind and the body. The authority of the law does not extend so far, and what authority it does have, absent the faith, it possesses only weakly. So he who disturbs the faith received by all from of old (to return to my original argument) disturbs the very foundations of the Republic. His sin in this regard is all the greater, in so far as that which the Lord God deigned give the Republic for its reformation, he, by his imprudent actions, employs to its detriment. It seemed necessary to me to pause a bit and consider this, to speak of our disaccord, because those people upon whom such things depend, don't wish to understand with what grave danger to the Republic this quarrel in the matter of faith is associated. And secondly, so that those people who are the cause of such discord among people should see that in their goal of multiplying the glory of the Lord, at which they say that they are aiming, they miss the mark entirely, because they are just sowing dissension among the people, the result of which is a certain decline and fall toward which, as I have said from the start, our Republic is tending. Now, what sort of praise shall redound to the Lord from the destruction of the Republic, this I know not. I don't know what they're thinking. I can see nothing more than how in those countries today such as Egypt, Asia, Greece, and in all those realms that have been wrested from Christians by pagans, the true praise of the Lord has been cast out of the churches, and replaced by the faith of Mahomet.

LANDOWNER
We should ask them who they prefer: Mahomet or the pope.

RECTOR
I've no doubt but there'd be more than a few who'd call out to Pilate, *Dimitte nobis Barabbam*. But I think it's time for us to enter into the heart of the matter and for me to explain fully why I fear for our Republic.

LANDOWNER
Please do. That's what I'd like to hear.

RECTOR
Well, it's not entirely a good sign, what the Satyr complains of concerning us — that we have departed from our ancient and praiseworthy

customs, in place of which we've begun to concern ourselves with excess, debauchery, whoring, gluttony, and such things as that. Now, listen to what wise men have to say of such an exchange. Cicero could not praise highly enough that line of Ennius' which reads: *Moribus antiquis stat res Romana virisque*, which means 'the Roman Republic stands by virtue of its ancient customs, and its men.' Which words (states Cicero), seem by virtue of their pithiness and truth to be oracular, for no such city could be founded, let alone endure for so long, so grandly, so piously and so comprehensively, where such men did not rule, nor will you find such men in cities where there are not such customs. And so back in those early days, the national traditions formed worthy men, and serious men preserved the traditional culture. But this age — if we consider the Republic as a beautiful painting, just a bit faded by age — not only neglects to refresh it in the colours in which it was created, it doesn't even touch it up so that the lines that make up its original image might be discernible. For tell me — what have we today from those ancient morals, by which, as he says, the Roman Republic stands? These have fallen into such neglect that, not only do we not practice them, we are not even familiar with them. And what am I to say of the people? For peoples have perished on account of an insufficiency of solid mores — a decline and a fall of which we must not only be aware, but beware on our own account. For it is our own actions, and not some misfortune that threatens us; being as we are a Republic in name only, having lost the essence of the thing itself. Hear now what that wise man, so honoured in his Republic, says of this blight on customs — that a gaggle of scheming and debauched manslaughterers wish to be called a Republic! And if Ennius speaks truly when he says that the Roman Republic stands on ancient customs, then Cicero too was not mistaken, suspecting that the fall of those ancient customs was to tear at the Republic as well. For already in his days, contempt for ancient customs led to quarrels among the Romans, and in them so many people were lost that it is a fright to hear. In the end they fell under a tyrant's power, from whom they were never able to free themselves later. And thus so great and so noble a Republic came to an end, so that not even a shadow of it was to remain. Thus it would not be right for us to take this debauchery and luxury of our days lightly, especially as we know just what mores they were that marked the men who first sounded and then so long sustained that famous Republic, for *regna iisdem artibus conserventur, quibus ab initio parantur.*[29] You may find in the ancient registries (that I call that time to mind) how much the royal bed clothing cost, how much the underlining of a caftan, how much wine when the king received guests; and what is recorded there does not seem much at all — which when we read today, who among us would not chuckle? So modestly did the Polish kings of those days live, that the simplest farmer would be ashamed to live so today. What are we to think of the carriage of the common men, when such was that of the kings? It's easy to see that people did not find their happiness or self-respect in long dinners and foreign drink, but rather in sobriety and moderation, so necessary to a chivalric people. There is no reason for us to be surprised at the fact that the old kings lived lives of moderation, and, consequently, the common people did so as well, in comparison to the wasteful times of today, for they held in contempt, as a stain upon the Republic, those things which we vaunt today. And as to their nobility of character — this I would not wish to assay in comparison with us. All histories sing the praises of the Roman Curius, who, seated at his campfire roasting a radish, deigned not even to cast a glance at all the magnificent gifts with which the Samnites wanted to barter peace with him. Supposedly our worthy kings, and certainly their subjects too, did the same — sitting in kitchens and servants' quarters — and yet they were fierce towards their enemies. But setting aside ancient customs, let us return to those of the present, on account of which, like Cicero, I am filled with evil foreboding on behalf of our fatherland. It seems to me that the Republic is somewhat similar to the human body. Because as people generally say, each person becomes unstable as death approaches, supposedly because (as physicians aver) the minds of men *sequuntur temperamentam corporis*,[30] which as long as it holds to the mean, and is not disturbed, the person in question holds to his wonted carriage and behaviour. But as soon as the unity and concord of the natural humours, on which life depends, begin to divide and decompose, then the behaviour of people must also change somewhat, for, as has already been stated, the flesh and the mind have an understanding between them. The same thing happens in a Republic. As long as it holds stately to its laws and legislation, people care for their offices and obligations.

---

29   Latin: Kingdoms are preserved by the same arts, which brought them into being.

30   Latin: Follow the disposition of the body.

But let the Republic weaken just a little, retreat somewhat from its wonted position, and a transformation of mores occurs. Where crimes are not followed by punishment, there debauchery and riot must reign; where office and position are for sale, you should not be surprised to find people greedy and avaricious. If there be no discipline and training among the youth, surplus and waste grow from their idleness. Where virtue finds no reward, there the urge to serve the Republic must be extinguished. Finally, so as to bring all this to a conclusion in a few words, where there is no longer any distinction between right and wrong, there you will find many more bad people than good. For we all of us have a natural inclination to evil, unless something keeps that in check. And what is it that should do so but the laws, and those who are the guardians of the laws? And, if they do not do this, we shall become like those frogs on the board in Aesop's fable. In one example, and in but a few words he expresses in his fairy-tale what other philosophers need volumes to explain concerning the mutability of Republics. For *contemptus legum*[31] arises from the carelessness of our superiors, and he who does not wish to live under the rule of law must end up under a tyrant's rule. There is the bridle for riot — otherwise the lawless would not be withheld from anything — like the Giants in ancient times, who would challenge God in Heaven. Evil and arbitrary customs then, as has been sometimes said, are the cause of the perishing of Republics. And the cause of these evil customs is to be found in our corrupt nature, first, and then in the unconcern of the Republic itself, that is, the carelessness of our superiors, who fail to restrain arbitrary and licentious people in time, or who themselves give bad examples by their avaricious acquisition of wealth, and in all other areas of life.

LANDOWNER

But how is the Republic harmed if I myself am greedy or a wastrel? Of course, as far as losses are concerned, I am discommoded more than any other by that; but the greedy man is to be blamed for wanting to be at ease?

RECTOR

If only the greedy man had such restraint, that he only wished to be at ease, and could suffer a limit, but greed is never satisfied. Of course,

---

31   Latin: Contempt of the laws.

the more such a one has, the more he wants. So it is difficult to garnish the greedy with this excuse, that he just wishes to be at ease. For the time for that passed for him long ago. Just as greed has no limit or measure, so shall he never arrive at a comfortable wealth, for that's not what he's after, to be at his ease (which is based on the use of accumulated goods); rather, he wants to have more than anyone else, and what he has he will never put to use, nor set at the disposal of others for them to use. And here we see the truth of that verse: *Avarus nisi cum moritur nihil recte facit*, the greedy man never does well, they say, except in dying. The Republic is harmed by such greed, for it cannot endure except where there is virtue and propriety among the people, and these are both overturned by greed. For there is no lewd vice or unsightly deed to which greed and avarice will not induce a man. From this comes falsity, poison, murder, treason against one's lords and the surrender of fastnesses and cities into the hands of one's enemies. When Philip, King of Macedon, was told of an exceptionally strong, supposedly impregnable castle, he asked whether a path might not be found thereto for a mule bearing a chest of gold, signifying thereby that money is capable of conquering all things. Jugurtha was once a prisoner in Rome. Then, freed after winning over the first of the land by bribes and having his guilt absolved by gifts, he frequently repeated these words concerning Rome: 'It is a venal city, near calamity, if only a willing buyer be found.' In this same spirit Pontius Samnis (mentioned by Cicero) once said: 'If only Fortune had preserved me for such times when the Romans should begin to take gifts, I would put a swift end to their rule.' I might also call to mind here the case of our late lady the Queen, concerning whom an edict was passed to thwart her frequent trips Italy, according to which whoever dared accompany her on such a journey, if he were a nobleman, he would lose his nobility, if a peasant, he would lose his head. And a good edict it would have been — for then our present lord the King would not have to deal with the problems concerning Bari, which was an inheritance from her, his mother, nor with its being seized from him. But what came of it? That edict was in force for one day only. After the passage of one night, it was announced that, not only was it permitted to one and all to travel with the Queen, but that the King himself would reward at his own cost those who did. Why the quick about-face? What intrigue brought it about? It's hard to know, because the change occurred at night, and those who knew the reason, supposedly, are no longer among the living.

Yet the Queen herself, already on the road, said aloud to her people: *Si voluissem, et filium mihi vendidissent.* From such examples then, you may see in what danger that lord, and this Republic, find themselves, when people are greedy for gain, for to such people neither wife nor children, nor fatherland, nor God Himself is so dear as gold. And such are the wastrels, as I once heard tell of a certain one who, when he was asked 'What will you do when you've squandered quite all of your wealth?' he replied, 'I'll sing for my supper, strumming on my lute.' Now, if all were such as he, I could still suffer them. But what a scandal are they, *qui sua perdiderunt, cum deest, aliena sequuntur.*[32] And these cannot do otherwise but sow dissension, introduce chaos into the Republic, so that they might derive some advantage therefrom — as it is when something is ablaze, not all set themselves to the task of extinguishing the flames. Such a one in Rome was Catiline, who having consumed all that he had, wished to batten himself upon the Republic, and when his silent practices furthered not his aims, he departed the city, taking with him an army of those like unto him, and initiated a battle, which, as God willed, he lost. He remained on the battlefield alone, surrounded on this side and that by worthy Romans, and fell beneath the blows of all. So, wasteful people harm not only themselves, as you suggested; they do significant damage to the Republic as well, as this example teaches us. Such a danger faces the Republic from arbitrary and debauched persons, for they, holding law in contempt, contemn also the office and dignity of the throne, which, if they were threatened by the same, they would seek any and all manners of fomenting chaos and rebellion amongst the people so as to avoid it. And if they were unsuccessful at this at home, they would betray both fatherland and liege, taking themselves off to an enemy so as to bring fire and sword against their own homeland. History is full of such examples. People are led to such things by ambition. For where they cannot achieve their aims by stealthy practice, they resort either to general violence, or come to an understanding with foreign powers to evoke a revolt, and both of these paths lead to the downfall of the Republic. I hope that you now understand how bad and debauched morals harm the Republic.

---

32   Latin: Who lose what belongs to them, and when they do, chase after what belongs to others.

LANDOWNER

I understand you well, but I would hear more.

RECTOR

Well, then tell me. How does it seem to you — in this our dissent and debauchery, when our lord the King has no descendant who, although having no right to inherit the throne by primogeniture, still, — ought we not to hope that we should rather agree to the throne being entrusted to someone whose father and grandfather ruled over us in succession, than that we should seek a king elsewhere, in foreign parts?

LANDOWNER

We may well hope indeed, and such a thing has been discussed at several diets. But as it is with us, proposals are an easy thing to make, but harder to bring to a conclusion.

RECTOR

For whom do the delegates vote at such times?

LANDOWNER

Each votes for his own.

RECTOR

And so they will again, should the occasion arise. God only knows how the final agreement would turn out. Good Lord in Heaven, preserve His Majesty for many years yet! But look on, further — see how the road is being paved toward misfortune. Our ancestors had wisely provided for the order of our Republic during an *interregnum*: they made the Primate, the Archbishop of Gniezno, regent, with power to convene a Diet, at which the new king would be elected and crowned. But who respects the archbishop today? Are we all going to heed his words? — They call him the servant of the Antichrist. God forbid we obey him in anything at all! And if there is to be such disorder that we withdraw from this ancient custom of ours (God grant that I am mistaken here) — before we elect a king, we will have more than one of them! No better symptom of our disorder might be found than this, that so large a kingdom as ours, set between such great enemies, has no Hetman! You wouldn't even allow the office of a village mayor to remain vacant for so long. We are too bold in this, we dare too much! That Italian spoke the truth when he declared that *sorte in Polonia vivitur.*[33] But should danger suddenly fall upon us, then shall we go looking for a military leader. And God grant that we find him then. Add to this the neglect of our needed fortresses — unprepared, allowed to fall into ruin. That's no good thing, is it? For in time of necessity, where shall they run for cover with their wives and children? We might have learned our lesson from Połock, which was lost through our neglect — if only God willed that we should recover it as easily as we lost it. But I doubt it. Listen further! Some lines from an ancient comedy come to my mind, which Cicero once quoted, and which seem fitting to our situation, as they refer to the fall of a Republic. So one person asks *Quaeso, qui vestram rempublicam tam cito amisistis?* And the reply he gets in response: *Proveniebant oratores novi, stulti, adolescentuli.*[34]

LANDOWNER

Is he not speaking of our representatives here?

RECTOR

If you wish to replace 'orators' with 'representatives.'

LANDOWNER

Well? Is it not thus that they are termed by the chancellery: *oratori nostro,* 'to our representative'?

RECTOR

True enough. But in this place (as I assume you know yourself) mention is not being made of representatives. But indeed we might learn from this verse: woe to that Republic, where such people as the poet describes gather in council, and especially where they shall be so numerous that one might say of them *proveniebant oratores.* There's also a verse in Homer that I call to mind: 'It's a bad thing where many govern; let there be but one king.' And one of the Emperors said as he

---

33   Latin: One lives by chance in Poland.

34   Latin: Please, what was it that led your Republic to ruin so quickly? The advent of new, stupid, young orators.

was dying, that *multitudo medicorum occident principem*.[35] God forbid that something of the sort should be said later of our Republic.

LANDOWNER

I agree with you that it's bad when there are many rulers. It's better when they are few, and wise.

RECTOR

Now, will you allow me to repeat what Plato says somewhere, that a change in music brings with it a change in the Republic?

LANDOWNER

That's too difficult for me.

RECTOR

All of the ancient philosophers were in agreement on this point, that music has a power over the human mind, and among the other exercises imposed on the youth they also required of them familiarity with music, as much for sober enjoyment and pleasant pastime, as for the establishment of good morals; for this reason too was music introduced into the churches, so as to excite the piety of the congregation. This is something that these new prophets don't consider, who, whenever they hear an organ they imagine it to indicate profane dancing. And with this sort of preaching they make proper churches repugnant to the simple people, as if music were for nothing more than that, as it was for that Luther before he turned from mincing fellow to minister. Now the men of old had such measures, or, to borrow their own term, harmonies, that so played on the emotions that, as they say of Alexander — as soon as he heard the band strike up, he leapt from table and called for arms. Pythagoras too, becoming aware of an irate youngster who was setting off to wreak violence upon a certain woman at her home, had them play a *spondaeum* (as they called it) and this so soothed him that, growing calm, he went away without doing any harm. So, when the music that acts as a leader to our emotions changes, then do the people's manners change, and as manners change, so do the laws. And so, as we read in the histories, the famous musician Tymoteus was banished from Athens

---

35   Latin: The king is killed by a multitude of physicians.

for no other reason than his having added one additional string to his instrument. Yet in our day and age, not one string, but nine have been added to the lute, and today's songs are as different from 'Bogurodzica'[36] as our morals are from our statutes. So, such a change in music brings in its wake a transformation of the Republic, if we wish to take Plato's word for it — who wanted no poets in his Republic, for they are such as can direct the people's emotions at will.

LANDOWNER

I dare say nothing against Plato, for I hear that he was a learned man. But have you any other of these guesses of yours?

RECTOR

I'm not sure that I do. I'd just remind you that hardly a realm exists where this quarrelling over faith has been avoided, and rare is the kingdom that did not undergo a significant catastrophe on its account. Most recently France, and thereafter the Netherlands. I fear greatly lest this inferno should reach us, for *similes causae similes effectus* bring; we need to petition the Lord God fervently that He fill us with His Spirit. I'm glad that I thought of this, as I was just about to finish speaking — when I say this last, I shall have done. I understand that you've heard of a certain thing that bodes no good to our Crown in these days of ours, and so certain you may be of it, as if you beheld it with your very own eyes. In the Bishop's Palace in Poznań there is a great hall. There, before its renovation by the late Bishop Czarnkowski, all the Kings of Poland were painted in a row — as they supposedly still are today. After King Zygmunt there was space enough for only one more king's portrait. There, when it came time to paint our present lord's image on that space, which, as I say, was the last space remaining, as it was being inspected, they found inscribed above it on the plaster, by sword or knife, these words: *hic regnum mutabitur.*[37] No one knows who wrote it there or how they climbed up so high to do it, for it was found right

---

36   The oldest Polish hymn recorded. 'Bogurodzica' means 'Mother of God;' this Marian hymn, sung at the Battle of Grunwald in 1410, when the forces under King Władysław Jagiełło defeated those of the German Knights of the Cross, is the oldest Polish national anthem.

37   Latin: Here the kingdom will be changed.

beneath the rafters. It might be that whoever wrote the prophecy there derived it from the fact of there being only one more space remaining, and it might also have been an inspiration from elsewhere, of which we know nothing. Whatever the case may be, it is a certain fact that this was written there; it may be significant, and it may be without significance — I dare not speculate either way. But all the same it may be entered among all other prophecies, like any other, and the Lord God has the power to turn all to the good. Now I've said all that I understand concerning our Republic, and why I fear for it. Certainly, I might have thought it all out better and arranged it differently, but it couldn't be otherwise, given the time I had. Anyway, I won't be rushing off to the printer's with it.

LANDOWNER

Well, what you've said and deduced is that we Poles are in bad shape, amidst rising waters. So tell me, is it all over for us, are we to doubt entirely of our rescue, or is there still some hope?

RECTOR

If God aid us not, and if our determinations be not better, in vain may we expect any good issue of it all.

LANDOWNER

Then we should also speak of how to avoid this fall.

RECTOR

Is that not what is discussed at the Diets?

LANDOWNER

Of course. That and revenue, of which we are in such urgent need.

RECTOR

Those taxes you mention, as I see, haven't been good for much but to pull money and horses out of Poland, and to starve Lithuania.

LANDOWNER

It seems that all you can do is cast blame, which is easy enough. But if you could indicate the path to a repairing of our ills, that would be something wise.

RECTOR

And for that reason I'll keep my mouth shut, as I'm well aware of how far we are from wisdom. But some day I will say what I understand concerning it all. But not now. I reckon that I've spoken, and you've listened, long enough.

LANDOWNER

I agree. But whenever you wish to speak of these things, as you promise, I will always be happy to give ear to you.

PROSE

An Essay on Virtue

That Drunkenness is a Filthy Thing Beneath

the Dignity of Man

On Czech and Lech

A Pattern of Virtuous Women

Apophthegmata

An Essay on Virtue

We appreciate virtue even in enemies and strangers. But that word 'virtue' contains within it many things.

First of all, wisdom, which teaches us what ought to be sought out and defended.

Second, justice, which demands that we give to all what is due them.

Third, magnanimity, which depends on holding all things temporal in contempt.

Fourthly, modesty in both speech and action.

And from these four virtues, as from four wells, many other virtues are drawn, which correct human manners.

The reason is trained by learning, which has many branches. The first among these are chivalry and law, and following them, the liberal arts.

Two things, therefore, ennoble man: manners and intelligence. Manners come from the virtues, and reason from study; both of these things contain something invaluable to man. But if only one of these is to remain a man, let it be virtue he holds to, rather than learning. For learning without virtue is like a sword in the hands of a madman: he harms himself as well as others. Virtue, though it be accompanied by nothing else, is praiseworthy and useful.

So, people love virtue, and next to virtue, intelligence. They also love what is to their advantage. Now, you will attract the simple most quickly with generosity and gifts. But such a friend is not loyal, for he loves your gifts more than yourself, and when you shall have nothing to give him, your friend will also vanish, unless he be one of those who remember good things done unto them — and such men are small in number, indeed.

Thus, two things are needed in this regard. First, that you should give so that you would always have a surplus. Second, that you should give to them who are worthy of such gifts, for doing good unto the good, you do good unto yourself.

JAN KOCHANOWSKI

But a man can be helpful to another with words as well, as when he advises him in his need; when he warns him away from an unbecoming thing; for all such actions, a man is beloved.

A third manner is to be willing to praise another, when such is pleasing to him, but here one must take great care never to offend against virtue or propriety in so doing. If you wish to have a friend, it is well not to praise him to his face as you do before others.

Now, it is quite improbable for anyone to be able to please all people (for that which pleases one man repulses another). It will be enough if he who wishes to be regarded as pleasant should preserve virtue and propriety in all things, whereby all should rightly love him. And if such be not the result of his actions, it will not be his fault (as he did all that he could), but rather the fault of those who do not love virtue.

But nor is it good to have too many friends. For when love is torn into little portions it is not as strong as that which is reciprocally held and cohesive; and he who loves but little, is loved but little in return.

So my advice is that a person have few friends, but such as are completely worthy of trust: such as Pylades and Orestes, Prithous and Theseus, Damon and Pythias, Scipio and Scaevola.

To get such friends — although what we have said above serves that end well — this needs special discernment, and requires much time, above all — it is important as far as virtue is concerned that no friend be set above the altar, as the Greek saying goes.

Common manners, and also common interests, usually attract one person to another. Thus soldier is always drawn to soldier, huntsman to huntsman.

But just as is the case with gold, which is proved in the fire, thus our friends are proved in need. And so, when aught befalls a comrade, think: now is the time and opportunity provided you to show just what sort of friend you are. For the flatterer will follow you like your shadow in bright sunlight as long as you be in good fortune, but should that good fortune ever change, then, just as when a cloud passes overhead and your shadow disappears, so too will he vanish without a trace. Thus, it befits the true friend to stand firmly beside his comrade, holding Fortune, which is ever fickle, in contempt.

But because virtue is the foundation of friendship, let a man first take care that he be the best he can be. Then, being good himself, let him seek the friendship of the good. The indolent, the spendthrift, the greedy, the quarrelsome — these are bad friends. Beneficence, hope, love, learning, agreeableness, willingness to praise — all these win us the love of others.

What did Hercules ever do in order to be loved?

There are two things that bring about love in people: the thing itself, love, for love attracts love, and that which is worthy of being loved.

That Drunkenness is a Filthy Thing

Beneath the Dignity of Man (1585)

I offer something unusual for your consideration: I well understand that not everyone will listen to me gladly. But if I speak the truth, well, let each man judge me as he sees fit. I have such hope that people who are reasonable and capable of distinguishing between dignity and filth will take my side. Indeed, I find myself unable to praise excess of any kind, but especially the gravest of all: when people speak of something so obviously worthless in wondrous terms, and something for which they ought actually to be ashamed, they take as something not only desirable, but even worth chasing after. Let us set aside such things, however many they be, if there be anything under the sun so filthy as drunkenness, and speak rather of it — on account of which both man and God, one's own obligations, and, in the end, even one's self, are neglected. Yet people always so sugar-coat it that no banquet, no droll entertainment can be imagined without drunkenness being a part thereof; this is the sort of behaviour they seek to indulge in, in such a way do they wish to please others. And yet each one who so acts shows great dislike for his very nature, veritably putting on display his ingratitude and displeasure at being created a man by God, rather than a beast. For if he is grateful and happy to see himself human, why then does he voluntarily stifle his reason by drunkenness, that very reason that differentiates him from the animals? Why does he cast away his wit and rationality, which exceeds that of other animals, by such excessive gluttony? I need not much to prove the insanity of such people; let them tell us themselves, if they can remember anything, what was going on with them yesterday. They even use drink as an excuse for the quarrels they engage in, saying that 'it was because they were drunk.' So, all the more deserving are you of punishment, for having done harm to your neighbour as well as yourself, because you were drunk! Much harm and insult is done to peaceful people by the insane, who have lost their reason either because of serious illness or on account of great trouble and worry, but in such cases, people treat them with understanding, and are more saddened by this woe suffered by their neighbours than they are at their own harm caused by them. But the drunken man has no such reasonable justification, nor can he have, for there is no other cause of his insanity, no accident or punishment of God, but his own desire, his own free will and evil habit that is to blame. Who is able to count up the many quarrels, murders, and so many other shameful things that occur on account of excessive, unbridled drunkenness? Things that would never occur to a man when he is sober — these he commits when drunk. There is no filthy thing that the drunken man would be ashamed of doing. There is no thing too disgusting for him to attempt. It's all one to him; God Himself must sometimes bear his violence. And what profit they obtain from it all is clear to the eyes of everyone. Nature herself seems to enact punishment on her ungrateful sons: this one is punished in his hand, that one upon his legs — this one grows swollen, that one begins to rot — they are either covered in boils or go leprous — there is not a single healthy one among them; they are overthrown entirely, undone to the death by illness or under the blows of others. In such varied liveries does common excess colour her courtiers; in such threads does she clothe them; thus does she pay her servants. The thing that fills me with most wonder is that, although they clearly see that they are overpaying for all this with their health, people still curtail not their excesses nor in any manner do they wish to follow measure in any thing, although this would help them to preserve both reason and full health. For when is it that people best see to their duties, and fulfil them? Only when they are sober. When is their wit sharpest in all things? Only when they have not overcome it with food or drink. Truly, just as the sun loses its lustre when it is covered by clouds, so man's reason is dulled when overcome by excess. And the strangest thing of all is, at such times a person thinks himself wisest when he is filthiest, bravest and strongest when he is weakest — so little is required to impair reason either by a lack or the perversion of the same. But sobriety, which makes our reason fully conscious of both its strengths and its weaknesses, will never lead a man into something of which he is incapable; rather, sooner will it retain its dignity (of which reason is the very foundation) by holding its tongue than by urging a man to attempt something beyond his means. Oh, the reason is a thing invaluable, although at times it may be found in a weak or deficient body. For by its counsel it can aid a man better than the greatest, stupid strength. Of what praise is such a virtue unworthy, the preservation of which ensures not only the health of our minds, but also guarantees us strength in fulness? Sobriety and measure are the most faithful guardians of our health. With their aid, man is able not only to avoid many grave illnesses, but also to cure himself of some. The first step to becoming healthy, to curing all illnesses, is a life led modestly and in proper measure. In short, that one virtue paves the way for all the rest. So is the reason of man and his mind strengthened thereby, that all honest science, all virtue, is easily assimilable — all the things from which drunkenness cuts one off, by setting up obstacles on the road thereto. I stand by this virtue; I confess to it. Let anyone say whatever he please about this attitude! I much prefer to ascribe to it than to drunkenness. For I do not believe that such a true friend might ever play one false; no, into his hands one can confide oneself securely. And as the common saying goes: the company you keep becomes second nature. Virtue and gentle manners draw people together. I see nothing of the sort in drunkenness that should attract the well-bred man, but rather, only such things as should rightly disgust him. But now you'll say to me: You got used to that in Italy. Sure! It wasn't among the Germans, who are just as gluttonous as we are. If you don't want to imitate the Italians, well, you'll find the same sort of moderate behaviour amongst the Turks, whom you take for pagans. But the reasonable man is not to behave in a certain way just because he sees others doing so, but because it is fitting. I'm not saying that anyone should imitate foreign manners — just that he should consider them. And if such manners are in accord with virtue and reason, why should you not imitate them? Don't do anything just because Italians and Spaniards do, but because so your duty directs you. Sugar-coat drunkenness as you will, you will always find moderation opposed to it. And if I call moderation a virtue (and who will forbid me from doing so?) let me challenge you here and now to find for yourself a proper and fitting name for drunkenness!

ON CZECH AND LECH

Just as nearly all other nations derive their beginnings more from fable than anything certain, so too the Polish nation is none too sure concerning its ancestors. For setting Noah aside along with all the other genealogies through which the Slavic nation winds its errant and doubtful way — those brothers Czech and Lech, which the chronicles offer us as the surest ancestors of us and the Czechs, bring with them enough baggage of doubt that their descendants may not so obviously recognise their protoplasts in them. First of all, we don't find these two Slavic chiefs, Lech and Czech, mentioned in the works of any foreign historian who speaks of the Slavs (save for such as base their accounts on our own). And it's not just that we don't find them in the works of foreign historians, for Kadłubski,[38] who, being a Pole, composed his Polish chronicle, makes no mention of either of them in his history, as far as I can recall. Later, those who set this Lech and Czech on their feet, so baselessly support their surmises as to be unable to mention any son or descendant of them by name. Moreover, they relate their deeds in such a murky way that nothing but their own boldness and ignorance is put on display. Despite all this, those that do indeed state that our nations only received their names from Czech and Lech after they had arrived in these lands, ought to tell us what they were called before they got here, since every Slavic nation has always been known by its own name, such as the Bulgars, the Serbs, the Slovaks, and many others, by which historians have known them since time immemorial. And since it is not the case with those who speak of Czech and Lech, I'm not sure to what extent we may believe them. For it is not a probable thing at all that two such great nations, who founded two kingdoms, being, after all, newcomers in their lands, were not to possess their own names until such

---

38   Bl. Wincenty Kadłubek (c. 1150–1223), Cistercian, Bishop of Kraków, author of the *Historia Poloniae* [History of Poland], c. 1210.

time as Czech and Lech appeared on the scene. And they only showed up when these lands were settled by others, who chose them for their homelands. Now, although someone might say that they were Slovaks, this doesn't hold water. For the Slovaks[39] continued on past the Danube to settle on the shores of the sea near Venice, where they remain until this day, in a land named after them: Slavonia. Now, that the Poles, like the Czechs, and the Rus in Moscow, as well as many other nations, are known as Slavs, this arises from the fact that the historians first came to know the Slovaks and introduced them, so to speak, to the world. And so, whoever spoke the Slavic tongue was taken for a Slovak, and thus the common name 'Slav' began to be applied to all nations employing this language. But again, just as the Czechs, the Russians, the Bulgars, and the Serbs or Sorabi, so the Slovaks, though speaking the same tongue, are a different and distinct nation, which, as I say above, crossed the Danube and settled in Illyria. And so, the Czechs and the Poles were never rightly Slovaks, who later rechristened themselves Czechs and Lachs. For that which some aver, that Czech and Lech came from the Slavic lands, or, as they call it, from Croatia, is nothing but a fairy story. For the Slovaks themselves originated in these northern lands, as we learn from actual history. Nor is it probable that so numerous a people, as are these two nations, were to be found in so small a land as Croatia. And what are we to say about the Russians — just as populous a nation, or those Slavs who inhabit the Baltic shores around Gdańsk? Did they also once live in Croatia before moving out? It is a much more probable thing then, that that handful of people splintered off from this great mass here, so to speak, and wandered there. And so, seeing as our fore-fathers did not come from Slavonia, nor were they Slovaks. And if they were not Slovaks, and the names of the modern nations were only, at last, derived from Czech and Lech, they had to be called something else beforehand, names they bore from their earliest days. Nothing about any Lachs can be found in any ancient histories. And just as the Czechs do not derive from Czech, it seems, who is of rather recent date, so too

---

39   Kochanowski seems to conflate the Slovaks with the Slovenes here, and what follows. However, that the Slovaks did have an influence on the Southern as well as the Western Slavs, can be proven on the basis of linguistic affinities with the Illyrian Slavs, as well as the Western Slavs (Poles and Czechs) with whom they are grouped and are most akin.

the Lachs most likely possessed that name earlier than the appearance of his brother Lech. To feel out the truth in this matter, especially as we possess no written record, is a difficult thing to do.

Every Slavic nation calls a Czech a Czech; only the Russians refer to Poles as Lachs. Can this be something of a shortening of the word *Polak* to the final syllable, with the thickening of the final consonant? Or is it because of our *latska* faith, i.e. Latin, since they themselves are Greek, that they term us Lachy, and according to that etymology, as Czech comes from *czeski*, *Włoch* from *włoski*,[40] so Lach is taken from *latski*, these last two letters, *s* or *ts*, standing in for the Greek *x*? So then, as a Czech has always been a Czech, so a Lach has always been a Lach, even though we, and nearly all nations following us, have stifled that old name with our new one, that is, *Polacy*, Poles — while the Russians halt where they were and continue to call us Lachs and not Poles, to this very day? And so, just as the Greeks term all the nations in the direction of the setting sun *Latinos*, so too the Russians, following their example, also call us *Włachy* (as do the Greeks) and, cutting away that first letter, Lachs? Procopius of Caesaria, the renowned historian, writing of the Caucasus and the frontiers of Byzantium, notes: 'Here, among other nations, the Alani and Abazgi live, and the Cekki and the Hunni, who are also known as Saberi.' Upon reading these words, we might assume that our own Czechs originated in these Cekki, especially considering the fact that all the nations he names here wandered later into Europe and settled on lands near the Danube — and so, along with them, these Cekki set out, eventually settling in Germany. But given the vastness of the Slavic nation I would not dare to state that all arose from a common source, unless the Alani and the Abazgi too spoke that language, for the Hunni are different. All these nations named here arrived — some at the Danube, others to the West; there is no need to doubt that if we were not known as Lachs in antiquity, then we most definitely had a different name in place of that, for we constituted one nation with the Czechs, splitting from them in time. For the name 'Pole' is a new one, and only arose in these regions on accord of the word *pole* [field], certainly with regard to others who inhabited forests or mountains or valleys, and who derive their names from those places. And though, as I see it, there is no small probability that the Czechs were always called Czechs and that

---

40   Polish: Italian.

JAN KOCHANOWSKI

the Polish nation was earlier known as Lachs, still it might have been that they lost their old name if, before 'Lech,' they had such, becoming known as Lachs later from someone in these lands known as Lech. For it is not for nothing that in our histories several princes are named Leszek as if the lesser 'Leszki' derived their name from some great Lech, appearing afterwards under his name and, in a fashion, resurrecting their ancestor.

A Pattern of Virtuous Women

(FRAGMENTS)

EVE

Eve, the mother of all generations, properly claims pride of place in these histories. And this is not on account of antiquity or because she precedes all other people in time, but because of her wondrous beginnings and extraordinary creation. For the fair sex has this to boast of in contrast to the male, in that she is not formed of the mud as was Adam, but, as Moses writes, of pure bone taken from his side. Whoever should like to know more of the creation of our first parents beyond what might be divined from the simple words of Moses, let him read, among other things, the second dialogue of the learned Jew Leon,[41] where he deduces that Plato derived his androgyne from this passage in Moses' writings. Now, whether or not this is to be believed is not for us to judge in this our present undertaking.

CHIOMARA

Chiomara, the wife of a certain Ortiagon, was captured at the time when the Romans smote the Galatians in Asia. During the division of spoils, she fell to the portion of a certain captain of horse, who treated her as he thought he had a right to do. Now, since in him immoderation met with greed, he decided to set a ransom for her after being approached by her friends wishing to redeem her. At the appointed time, the relatives of the lady received her from his hands after having set the ransom money before him. Wishing to display some humanity, the captain

---

41   Jehudah Abravanele (Abrabanel, fl. c. 1465–1520). Jewish philosopher, who took the name Leon after converting to Catholicism. The work referred to here is his *Dialogues on Love*; Plato's myth of the androgyne can be found in his *Symposium*.

of horse accompanied her himself to the spot on the river bank from which she was to cross over. Now she, not caring a jot for his present courtesy as she was mindful of the shame to which he had first subjected her, commanded her servant in whispered terms to kill him. When the opportunity provided itself, that servant carried out his mistress' wishes. Then she, severing the head from the trunk of the corpse, wrapped it up in some fabric and in this way carried it along with her. At last, when she stood before her husband, she cast it at his feet. At first, he was affrighted. But then, becoming well aware of all that had transpired, he asked his wife if it was a proper thing to place one's trust in anyone? 'Of course,' she replied. 'But it is even a more proper thing that, of the two men who have occupied my bed, only one should remain alive.'

ARISTOCLEA

A certain Theophanes had a daughter by the name of Aristoclea, who was beloved of two young men, Strato and Callisthenes. Strato was the wealthier of the two and loved the girl more. Callisthenes, on the other hand, was endowed with greater grace, and was in a way related to her. Now, it being the case that the girl's father feared the one more than the other, he decided to consult the bards of Apollo as to which he was to accept as his son-in-law. But Strato, having learned from the household servants that the girl was more inclined to him than to Callisthenes, urged that she be allowed to choose her husband for herself. Later, when Theophanes asked the girl, in the presence of everyone, to choose, and her choice fell upon Callisthenes, it was immediately apparent that Strato was greatly insulted thereby. A few days after this, Strato arrived at Theophanes' home, where he found Callisthenes present as well. He promised them both that, although he had met with misfortune, some-how, in this matter of a wife, still, as before, he wished to remain friends with both men. In reply, they invited him to the wedding. He promised to be there, but first made sure to gather together as many companions and servants toward that day as possible. These he imperceptibly scat-tered among the crowds, bidding them to await his signal. And when the maiden was led forth to be wed, he gave his helpers the sign they were waiting for, and threw himself upon her. Seeing this, Callisthenes strove to tear her from him by force. Servants on both sides rushed to aid their respective masters, but the girl, being so violently torn this way and that, gave up the ghost. Upon seeing this, Callisthenes disappeared from the eyes of man and no one ever saw or heard of him again. Strato, on the other hand, standing over the dead maiden, slew himself with his own hand in the sight of all.

KAMMA

Once, there were two illustrious youths in Galatia, Sinatus and Sinoryx, equal to each other in upbringing and wealth, who lived on terms of sincere amity. One of these two, Sinatus, took a wife by the name of Kamma, a woman who towered above all other females of the time both in beauty and honesty. Sinoryx fell head over heels in love with her. But since he could not sway her to his use by entreaties, nor could he even consider employing force as long as Sinatus was among the living, he took impious counsel and arranged in secret for Sinatus to be murdered. After the killing, he sent intermediaries to Kamma with proposals of marriage. Now she, knowing well who was to blame for her orphaned state, set to thinking how she might avenge the spilling of her husband's innocent blood. And since Sinoryx knew no measure in his demands, and his friends were ceaselessly hounding her to accept him, and not to hold his amity in contempt, she let herself be swayed and sent word that he should come to the church where they would be married. As soon as he arrived, she greeted him gracefully and led him to the altar. There, taking in hand a golden chalice, and performing a libation according to the rites of pagan Diana, she drank first from the chalice and then gave the remainder to Sinoryx. The chalice held poison. When he had drunk it down, she knelt at the altar and said the following: 'I here declare to thee, most renowned goddess, that following the death of my husband I have lived on only in expectation of this very day. For, having lost nearly half of my own soul, what might have kept me among the living save my hopes of the vengeance I exact today? And now that with thy aid I have accomplished what I so longed for, gaily rejoicing, I go to join my husband. And as for you, you evil man — not marriage-bed, but grave shall be your portion, and instead of a wedding, your friends and relatives will now be preparing your funeral.' Upon hearing these words, and sensing the poison begin to work in him, he raced out of the church in terror. But, unable to find any antidote for the poison, he died that same night after long hours of torment. And God granted Kamma such comfort, that she herself did not expire until word came to her of the death of her enemy.

TIMOCLEA

When Alexander, the King of Macedon, had taken Thebes by force, his soldiers set about their looting. The house of Timoclea, of whom we are now to speak, was occupied by one of Alexander's chief generals. He made himself at home there, living according to the dictates of his fancy, but he took no notice of Timoclea herself. He was most interested in money. Desirous of learning whether she had buried any coin or other treasure, he strove to elicit information from her, now by threats, now by gentle words. But she, prudent woman that she was, planned on discovering a way in which to wreak vengeance upon her enemy despite her weakness. So, she told him that she had deposited all of her treasures in a cavern in her garden. The greedy man made her lead him to that cavern, and, seeing that it would not be difficult to lower himself down inside it, did so. When Timoclea was certain that he had reached the very bottom, she began to pelt him so thickly with stones that he could in no way make his exit by the same route. She threw in so many stones as nearly to bury him alive. When news of this spread on the next day, Timoclea was apprehended and led before the king. Taking note both of her beauty and the dignity of her expression, the king inquired as to who she might be. She answered him in such words: 'My name is Timoclea. I am the sister of Teagenes, who, lately warring against you on behalf of the liberty of all Greece, fell in battle so that we might avoid what has now befallen us. And because I have been subjected to such shame today, such as my family has never before known, I do not seek to avoid death; rather, I prefer to die now rather than to spend another such night waiting.' The king was astonished at the heart and reasoning of that stately woman, and on her account proclaimed that no harm should be done to honest households. He then set Timoclea at liberty and commanded that she, and all her relations live henceforth unmolested.

MIKKA

Aristotimus, tyrant of Elis, appointed by King Antigonus, treated his people harshly and impiously. Amongst his injustices and crimes, he is notorious for how he dealt with Philodemos. Now, Philodemos had a daughter named Mikka, who had caught the eye of a certain Lucius, who was the tyrant's courtier. He sent his servant to fetch the girl for him. Her father and mother, gripped with fear, took counsel what they should do, but Mikka fell to her knees before her father and begged him, for God's sake, rather to see her dead than living in shame. Now Lucius, noting that his envoy was long in returning, went off himself to Philodemos' house, not entirely sober. When he came upon the girl on her knees before her father, he commanded her, with threats, to go with him, and since she was none too eager to comply, he tore the clothes she was wearing into tatters and beat her cruelly. Looking upon so heartbreaking a scene, and seeing that their pleas went unheeded, her father and mother lifted their voices to the heavens, calling upon God to aid them. Lucius, meanwhile, overheated both with wine and fury, slew the innocent girl before her parents' very eyes. Aristotimus was unmoved by the event, and even sent to their own deaths many of those who came complaining to him of this injustice. Others he banished from the city — some four hundred left for Aetolia. But although they often begged him to allow their wives and children to follow them into exile, their suits were never granted.

APOPHTHEGMATA

(FRAGMENTS)

BAD IDEA: TO PUT TWO CATS INTO THE SAME SACK

A certain royal chancellor was in the habit of saying, 'I can get along with anyone except a greedy man, because he's after the same things as me.'

AN UNPREMEDITATED RECONCILIATION

Archbishop Gamrat was angry with Father Krupski. One day it so fell out that the archbishop was riding from the castle in Kraków, at the same time as Father Krupski was riding to it. They happened to meet up with one another right in front of the archbishop's palace. Now, Father Krupski's horse had such a habit that, when he came across another of his kind, it was difficult to draw him away. It often occurred that, should he meet another horse along his way, he would gladly turn around and follow the other horse, going back the way he had just come. This is exactly what happened at the moment in question. Now, Father Krupski would have been more than happy to give the archbishop a wide berth and pass him by, and yet that nag of his just stood stock still and began nuzzling and tangling with the archbishop's horse so, that there was simply no way of pulling her aside, and the result was that the priest's horse followed the other right through the archway and into courtyard of the archbishop's palace, carrying Father Krupski with him, of course, trembling with fear and worry. At first, the archbishop was angry. But then, when he understood what had just happened, he began to laugh uproariously. He invited Father Krupski to dinner, at which the two men were reconciled.

UNNECESSARY CEREMONIES

Whenever it chanced that a toast was to be raised to someone present at his table, Father Myszkowski, the Bishop of Płock, would request that all remain seated while the toast was raised, or, if anyone insisted on getting up, at least it should only be the one who raised the toast, and the one being toasted. For what reason had anyone else to stand? 'When two people are toasting,' he would say, 'and a third one gets up as well, it's as if he were saying "Drink to me, too!"'

UNNATURAL NOURISHMENT

Baranczuch, a Tatar, was once given to a Cardinal in Rome as a gift by his master. A few years afterwards, he met by chance an old acquaintance who had come to Rome. When asked by the latter how he was faring, he replied, 'Poorly. Here you eat grass just like a sheep,'[42] by which he signified his dislike for Italian salad.

ON THE SAME

A certain Pole went off to university in Italy. He stayed through the summer only, returning home when the weather turned cold. When his father asked him why he'd come back so quickly, he replied: 'All they gave me to eat, all summer long, was grass. If that's how they feed a person in the summer, I was afraid that all I'd get in winter would be hay.'

A LORD'S JEST

Once, King Zygmunt was playing *flus*. Laying down his hand, which contained a pair of kings, he said 'Three kings.' When the other players asked 'Where's the third?' he replied 'Here,' pointing to himself. Needless to say, he won the hand.

---

42   The name 'Baranczuch' derives from *baran*, the Polish word for 'ram, sheep.'

THE UNCERTAIN CREDITOR

Archbishop Gamrat was a generous man, and, as a consequence, he was also frequently in debt. Once, upon being reminded by someone that he might want to give some thought as to how he would pay back a creditor, he replied, 'I had to give a lot of thought to how I would get the money in the first place; now let him give some thought as to how he's going to recoup it.'

THE SAME

The archbishop was indebted to X for a certain sum. Beginning to have his doubts concerning repayment, X began to visit the archbishop every day for dinner. When someone would ask him 'Where are you going?' he would reply, 'I'm going to eat another portion of my 500 złoty at the Archbishop's.'

LIARS

Stańczyk used to say that there were no two bigger liars in all of Poland than Archbishop Gamrat and Maciejowski the Bishop of Kraków. Because the former would say 'I know it all,' while knowing nothing, and the latter, 'Really, I know nothing at all,' while knowing everything there is to know.

AN UNEXPECTED ANSWER

A certain landowner in Poland took a wife. A few Sundays later, learning that his wife had gone into labour, he began to tear at the curtains in his distraction, at which she exclaimed, 'What are you getting so upset about? It's not even yours!'

[MONKS AND WIVES]

Siemieński, from the Radom area, lived a mile or so distant from the Benedictine monastery. He was well known for being extremely jealous of his wife, and, one day, during a banquet at his house, someone teased, 'It's said that the Tatars are raiding the land hereabout. What are we going to do with our wives and children, so as to keep them safe?' 'What about you?' one of them asked Siemieński. The neighbour at the table piped up with 'As for me, I can think of no better place than the monastery,' at which Siemieński said 'In that case, devil knows what to defend first — the city walls from the Tatars, or one's wife from the monks!'

[UNTIL THE LAST ASSIZES]

Dębieński, the royal chancellor, was once instructed by the King to adjourn a certain legal process, which at the time was being argued before the king's bench. So Dębieński announced, 'His Royal Highness the King has decreed that the matter in question shall be adjourned until the Judgement Day' — instead of the Assizes, or the day upon which the King himself was obliged to sit in judgement. In such a manner, it was thought, the chancellor, frustrated at the King's habits of procrastination, wished to make him aware of the exaggerated length of the continuance.

BIBLIOGRAPHY

PRIMARY SOURCES

KOCHANOWSKI, Jan. *Dzieła polskie*, ed. by Julian Krzyżanowski (Warsaw: Państwowy Instytut Wydawniczy, 1982).

KOCHANOWSKI, Jan. *Dzieła polskie*, Vol. I–III. (Warsaw: Państwowy Instytut Wydawniczy, 1953).

KOCHANOWSKI, Jan. *Dzieła wierszem i prozą, z popiersiem autora*, Vol. I. (Wrocław: Wilhelm Bogumił Korn, 1825).

SECONDARY SOURCES

CYTOWSKA, Maria. 'Kochanowski a Antyk (Tradycjonalizm czy nowatorstwo?,' in *Jan Kochanowski i Kultura Odrodzenia*, ed. by Zdzisław Libera and Maciej Żurowski (Warszawa: Państwowe Wydawnictwo Naukowe, 1985), pp. 90–106.

KRZYSZTOFORSKA-DOSCHEK, Jolanta. 'Polskie korzenie twórczości Jana Kochanowskiego,' *Wiener Slavistisches Jahrbuch*, Vol. 47 (2001), pp. 85–89.

LANGLADE, Jaques. 'Jan Kochanowski: L'humaniste,' *Revue des Etudes Slaves*, Vol. 10, No. 1/2 (1930), pp. 39–56.

MAGNUSZEWSKI, Józef. 'Twórczość Jana Kochanowskiego na tle poezji słowiańskiej XVI wieku,' in *Jan Kochanowski i Kultura Odrodzenia*, ed. by Zdzisław Libera and Maciej Żurowski (Warsaw: Państwowe Wydawnictwo Naukowe, 1985), pp. 121–130.

MATTAK, Janusz. 'Jan Kochanowski in Königsberg,' *Jahrbücher für Geschichte Osteuropas*, Vol. 36, No. 3 (1988), pp. 341–349.

MIŁOSZ, Czesław. *The History of Polish Literature* (Berkeley: University of California Press, 1983).

PARROTT, Ray J. 'Mythological Allusions in Kochanowski's Laments,' *The Polish Review*, Vol. 14, No. 1 (1969), pp. 3–19.

PELC, Janusz. 'Przemiany świadomości poetyckiej Jana Kochanowskiego,' in *Jan Kochanowski i Kultura Odrodzenia*, ed. by Zdzisław Libera and Maciej Żurowski (Warsaw: Państwowe Wydawnictwo Naukowe, 1985), pp. 58–75.

PIETRUSIEWICZOWA, Jadwiga and RYTEL, Jadwiga. 'Jan Kochanowski,' in Zdzisław Libera, et al. *Literatura Polska od średniowiecza do oświecenia* (Warsaw: Państwowe Wydawnictwo Naukowe, 1988), pp. 90–110.

PILAŘ, Jan. *Má cesta za polskou poezjí* (Prague: Československý spisovatel, 1981).

SROCZYŃSKI, Aleksander. 'We Were the Trojans Rhetoric and Political Community in Medieval and Early Modern Sarmatia and Illyria,' in *Premodern Rulership and Contemporary Political Power: The King's Body Never Dies*, ed. by Karolina Mroziewicz and Aleksander Sroczyński (Amsterdam: Amsterdam Univ. Press, 2017), pp. 169–192.

WALECKI, Wacław. 'Aus der Geschichte des altpolnischen Dramas (I. "Die Abfertigung der griechischen Sendboten" von Jan Kochanowski),' *Wiener Slavistisches Jahrbuch*, Vol. 33 (1987), pp. 167–173.

WEINTRAUB, Wiktor. 'Kochanowski's Renaissance Manifesto,' *The Slavonic and East European Review*, Vol. 30, No. 75 (1952), pp. 412–424.

WILSON, Reuel K. 'Kochanowski and Ronsard: Contemporaries and Kindred Spirits,' *The Polish Review*, Vol. 22, No. 1 (1977), pp. 19–28.

ZAREMBA, Charles, 'La disparition d'Ursule: Contribution à l'étude des Thrènes de Jan Kochanowski.' *Revue des Etudes Slaves*, Vol. 74, No. 2/3, Communications de la Délégation française au XIIIe Congrès international des slavistes (2002–2003), pp. 505–515.

ABOUT THE AUTHOR

Jan Kochanowski (1530–1584) is widely regarded as the greatest Slavic poet of the Renaissance period, and the greatest Polish poet until the advent of Adam Mickiewicz in the nineteenth century. Friend of Pierre Ronsard, widely travelled in Europe, Kochanowski created the modern poetic idiom in Polish, striving, like Horace before him (on whom he modelled his *Songs*), to achieve immortality through composing in his native language — although he also achieved a widespread fame in Europe for his Latin poems. He was creative in nearly all literary genres, and succeeded splendidly in each he attempted: lyric poetry, such as the *Songs* and the *Trifles*, drama (the humanist tragedy *The Dismissal of the Grecian Envoys*), translation (fragments of Euripides, the Greek Anthology, and Latin poets), narrative poetry (*The Satyr*), and prose. His greatest claim to fame is a cycle he never wished to write: the *Threnodies*, a cycle of laments written in honour of his daughter Orszula, who died not quite aged three.

ABOUT THE TRANSLATOR

Charles S. Kraszewski (born 1962) is a poet and translator, creative in both English and Polish. He is the author of three volumes of original verse in English (*Diet of Nails*; *Beast*; *Chanameed*), and two in Polish (*Hallo, Sztokholm*; *Skowycik*). He also authored a satirical novel *Accomplices, You Ask?* (San Francisco: Montag, 2021). He translates from Polish, Czech and Slovak into English, and from English and Spanish into Polish. He is a member of the Union of Polish Writers Abroad (London) and of the Association of Polish Writers (SPP, Kraków). In 2022 he was awarded the Gloria Artis medal (III Class) by the Ministry of Culture of the Republic of Poland. In 2023, he was awarded the ZAIKS prize for Translation into a Foreign Tongue by the Polish Author's Association (ZAIKS).

Acropolis – The Wawel Plays
by Stanisław Wyspiański

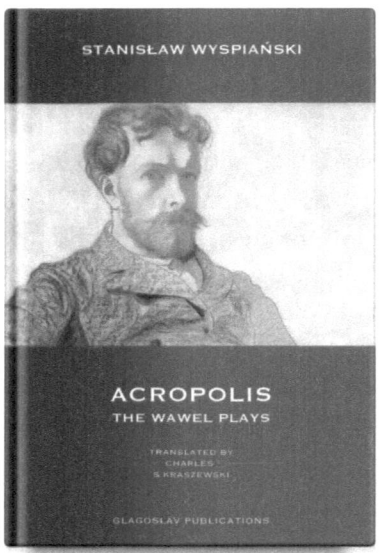

Stanisław Wyspiański (1869-1907) achieved worldwide fame, both as a painter, and Poland's greatest dramatist of the first half of the twentieth century. *Acropolis: the Wawel Plays*, brings together four of Wyspiański's most important dramatic works in a new English translation by Charles S. Kraszewski. All of the plays centre on Wawel Hill: the legendary seat of royal and ecclesiastical power in the poet's native city, the ancient capital of Poland. In these plays, Wyspiański explores the foundational myths of his nation: that of the self-sacrificial Wanda, and the struggle between King Bolesław the Bold and Bishop Stanisław Szczepanowski. In the eponymous play which brings the cycle to an end, Wyspiański carefully considers the value of myth to a nation without political autonomy, soaring in thought into an apocalyptic vision of the future. Richly illustrated with the poet's artwork, *Acropolis: the Wawel Plays* also contains Wyspiański's architectural proposal for the renovation of Wawel Hill, and a detailed critical introduction by the translator. In its plaited presentation of *Bolesław the Bold* and *Skałka*, the translation offers, for the first time, the two plays in the unified, composite format that the poet intended, but was prevented from carrying out by his untimely death.

Buy it > www.glagoslav.com

FOREFATHERS' EVE

by Adam Mickiewicz

Forefathers' Eve [*Dziady*] is a four-part dramatic work begun circa 1820 and completed in 1832 – with Part I published only after the poet's death, in 1860. The drama's title refers to *Dziady*, an ancient Slavic and Lithuanian feast commemorating the dead. This is the grand work of Polish literature, and it is one that elevates Mickiewicz to a position among the "great Europeans" such as Dante and Goethe.

With its Christian background of the Communion of the Saints, revenant spirits, and the interpenetration of the worlds of time and eternity, *Forefathers' Eve* speaks to men and women of all times and places. While it is a truly Polish work – Polish actors covet the role of Gustaw/Konrad in the same way that Anglophone actors covet that of Hamlet – it is one of the most universal works of literature written during the nineteenth century. It has been compared to Goethe's Faust – and rightfully so...

Buy it > www.glagoslav.com

Four Plays:

Mary Stuart, Kordian, Balladyna, Horsztyński

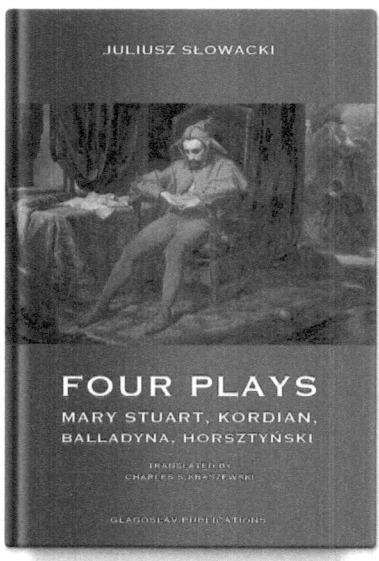

The dramas in Glagoslav's edition of *Four Plays* include some of the poet's greatest dramatic works, all written before age twenty-five: *Mary Stuart, Balladyna* and *Horsztyński* weave carefully crafted motifs from *King Lear, Macbeth, Hamlet* and *A Midsummer Night's Dream* in astoundingly original works, and *Kordian* — Słowacki's riposte to Mickiewicz's *Forefathers' Eve*, constitutes the final word in the revolutionary period of Polish Romanticism.

Translated into English by Charles S. Kraszewski, the *Four Plays* of Juliusz Słowacki will be of interest to aficionados of Polish Romanticism, Shakespeare, and theatre in general.

Buy it > www.glagoslav.com

Dramatic Works

by Zygmunt Krasiński

"God hath denied me that angelic measure / Without which no man sees in me the poet," writes Zygmunt Krasiński in one of his most recognisable lyrics. Yet while it may be true that his lyric output cannot rival in quality the verses of the other two great Polish Romantics, Adam Mickiewicz and Juliusz Słowacki, Krasiński's dramatic muse gives no ground to any other.

The Glagoslav edition of the *Dramatic Works* of Zygmunt Krasiński provides the English reader, for the first time, with all of Krasiński's plays in the translation of Charles S. Kraszewski. These include the sweeping costume drama Irydion, in which the author sets forth the grievances of his occupied nation through the fable of an uprising of Greeks and barbarians against the dissipated emperor Heliogabalus, and, of course, the monumental drama on which his international fame rests: the *Undivine Comedy*...

GŁOSY / VOICES

by Jan Polkowski

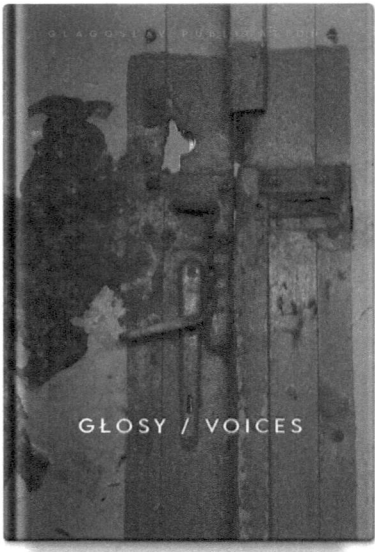

In December 1970, amid a harsh winter and an even harsher economic situation, the ruling communist regime in Poland chose to drastically raise prices on basic foodstuffs. Just before the Christmas holidays, for example, the price of fish, a staple of the traditional Christmas Eve meal, rose nearly 20%. Frustrated citizens took to the streets to protest, demanding the repeal of the price-hikes. Things took an especially dramatic turn in the northern regions near the Baltic shore — later, the cradle of the Solidarity movement, which would eventually spark the fall of communism in Poland and throughout Central and Eastern Europe — where the government moved against their citizens with the Militia and the Army. Forty-one Poles were murdered by their own government when militiamen and soldiers opened fire with live rounds on the crowds in Gdańsk, Gdynia, Szczecin and Elbląg.

Jan Polkowski's moving poetic cycle *Głosy* [Voices], presented here in its entirety in the English translation of C.S. Kraszewski, is a poetic monument to the dead, their families, and all who were affected by the 'December Events,' as they are sometimes euphemistically referred to.

A BILINGUAL EDITION

Buy it > www.glagoslav.com

OLANDA

by Rafał Wojasiński

I've been happy since the morning. Delighted, even. Everything seems so splendidly transient to me. That dust, from which thou art and unto which thou shalt return — it tempts me. And that's why I wander about these roads, these woods, among the nearby houses, from which waft the aromas of fried pork chops, chicken soup, fish, diapers, steamed potatoes for the pigs; I lose my eye-sight, and regain it again. I don't know what life is, Ola, but I'm holding on to it. Thus speaks the narrator of Rafał Wojasiński's novel *Olanda*. Awarded the prestigious Marek Nowakowski Prize for 2019, *Olanda* introduces us to a world we glimpse only through the window of our train, as we hurry from one important city to another: a provincial world of dilapidated farmhouses and sagging apartment blocks, overgrown cemeteries and village drunks; a world seemingly abandoned by God — and yet full of the basic human joy of life itself.

Buy it > www.glagoslav.com

- *A History of Belarus* by Lubov Bazan
- *Children's Fashion of the Russian Empire* by Alexander Vasiliev
- *Empire of Corruption: The Russian National Pastime* by Vladimir Soloviev
- *Heroes of the 90s: People and Money. The Modern History of Russian Capitalism* by Alexander Solovev, Vladislav Dorofeev and Valeria Bashkirova
- *Fifty Highlights from the Russian Literature* (Dutch Edition) by Maarten Tengbergen
- *Bajesvolk* (Dutch Edition) by Michail Chodorkovsky
- *Dagboek van Keizerin Alexandra* (Dutch Edition)
- *Myths about Russia* by Vladimir Medinskiy
- *Boris Yeltsin: The Decade that Shook the World* by Boris Minaev
- *A Man Of Change: A study of the political life of Boris Yeltsin*
- *Sberbank: The Rebirth of Russia's Financial Giant* by Evgeny Karasyuk
- *To Get Ukraine* by Oleksandr Shyshko
- *Asystole* by Oleg Pavlov
- *Gnedich* by Maria Rybakova
- *Marina Tsvetaeva: The Essential Poetry*
- *Multiple Personalities* by Tatyana Shcherbina
- *The Investigator* by Margarita Khemlin
- *The Exile* by Zinaida Tulub
- *Leo Tolstoy: Flight from Paradise* by Pavel Basinsky
- *Moscow in the 1930* by Natalia Gromova
- *Laurus* (Dutch edition) by Evgenij Vodolazkin
- *Prisoner* by Anna Nemzer
- *The Crime of Chernobyl: The Nuclear Goulag* by Wladimir Tchertkoff
- *Alpine Ballad* by Vasil Bykau
- *The Complete Correspondence of Hryhory Skovoroda*
- *The Tale of Aypi* by Ak Welsapar
- *Selected Poems* by Lydia Grigorieva
- *The Fantastic Worlds of Yuri Vynnychuk*
- *The Garden of Divine Songs and Collected Poetry of Hryhory Skovoroda*
- *Adventures in the Slavic Kitchen: A Book of Essays with Recipes* by Igor Klekh
- *Seven Signs of the Lion* by Michael M. Naydan

- *Forefathers' Eve* by Adam Mickiewicz
- *One-Two* by Igor Eliseev
- *Girls, be Good* by Bojan Babić
- *Time of the Octopus* by Anatoly Kucherena
- *The Grand Harmony* by Bohdan Ihor Antonych
- *The Selected Lyric Poetry Of Maksym Rylsky*
- *The Shining Light* by Galymkair Mutanov
- *The Frontier: 28 Contemporary Ukrainian Poets - An Anthology*
- *Acropolis: The Wawel Plays* by Stanisław Wyspiański
- *Contours of the City* by Attyla Mohylny
- *Conversations Before Silence: The Selected Poetry of Oles Ilchenko*
- *The Secret History of my Sojourn in Russia* by Jaroslav Hašek
- *Mirror Sand: An Anthology of Russian Short Poems*
- *Maybe We're Leaving* by Jan Balaban
- *Death of the Snake Catcher* by Ak Welsapar
- *A Brown Man in Russia* by Vijay Menon
- *Hard Times* by Ostap Vyshnia
- *The Flying Dutchman* by Anatoly Kudryavitsky
- *Nikolai Gumilev's Africa* by Nikolai Gumilev
- *Combustions* by Srđan Srdić
- *The Sonnets* by Adam Mickiewicz
- *Dramatic Works* by Zygmunt Krasiński
- *Four Plays* by Juliusz Słowacki
- *Little Zinnobers* by Elena Chizhova
- *We Are Building Capitalism! Moscow in Transition 1992-1997* by Robert Stephenson
- *The Nuremberg Trials* by Alexander Zvyagintsev
- *The Hemingway Game* by Evgeni Grishkovets
- *A Flame Out at Sea* by Dmitry Novikov
- *Jesus' Cat* by Grig
- *Want a Baby and Other Plays* by Sergei Tretyakov
- *Mikhail Bulgakov: The Life and Times* by Marietta Chudakova
- *Leonardo's Handwriting* by Dina Rubina
- *A Burglar of the Better Sort* by Tytus Czyżewski
- *The Mouseiad and other Mock Epics* by Ignacy Krasicki
- *Ravens before Noah* by Susanna Harutyunyan

- *An English Queen and Stalingrad* by Natalia Kulishenko
- *Point Zero* by Narek Malian
- *Absolute Zero* by Artem Chekh
- *Olanda* by Rafał Wojasiński
- *Robinsons* by Aram Pachyan
- *The Monastery* by Zakhar Prilepin
- *The Selected Poetry of Bohdan Rubchak: Songs of Love, Songs of Death, Songs of the Moon*
- *Mebet* by Alexander Grigorenko
- *The Orchestra* by Vladimir Gonik
- *Everyday Stories* by Mima Mihajlović
- *Slavdom* by Ľudovít Štúr
- *The Code of Civilization* by Vyacheslav Nikonov
- *Where Was the Angel Going?* by Jan Balaban
- *De Zwarte Kip* (Dutch Edition) by Antoni Pogorelski
- *Głosy / Voices* by Jan Polkowski
- *Sergei Tretyakov: A Revolutionary Writer in Stalin's Russia* by Robert Leach
- *Opstand* (Dutch Edition) by Władysław Reymont
- *Dramatic Works* by Cyprian Kamil Norwid
- *Children's First Book of Chess* by Natalie Shevando and Matthew McMillion
- *Precursor* by Vasyl Shevchuk
- *The Vow: A Requiem for the Fifties* by Jiří Kratochvil
- *De Bibliothecaris* (Dutch edition) by Mikhail Jelizarov
- *Subterranean Fire* by Natalka Bilotserkivets
- *Vladimir Vysotsky: Selected Works*
- *Behind the Silk Curtain* by Gulistan Khamzayeva
- *The Village Teacher and Other Stories* by Theodore Odrach
- *Duel* by Borys Antonenko-Davydovych
- *War Poems* by Alexander Korotko
- *Ballads and Romances* by Adam Mickiewicz
- *The Revolt of the Animals* by Wladyslaw Reymont
- *Poems about my Psychiatrist* by Andrzej Kotański
- *Liza's Waterfall: The hidden story of a Russian feminist* by Pavel Basinsky
- *Biography of Sergei Prokofiev* by Igor Vishnevetsky
  More coming . . .

GLAGOSLAV PUBLICATIONS
www.glagoslav.com

www.ingramcontent.com/pod-product-compliance
Lightning Source LLC
Chambersburg PA
CBHW030937210726
48290CB00007B/2218